Uzma Aslam Khan was ... London and Karachi befo... ...y in the United States. She is married, ...e and is at work on a second novel.

The Story of Noble Rot

Uzma Aslam Khan

PENGUIN BOOKS

Penguin Books India (P) Ltd., 11 Community Centre, Panchsheel Park, New Delhi 110 017, India
Penguin Books Ltd., 27 Wrights Lane, London W8 5TZ, UK
Penguin Putnam Inc., 375 Hudson Street, New York, NY 10014, USA
Penguin Books Australia Ltd., Ringwood, Victoria, Australia
Penguin Books Canada Ltd., 10 Alcorn Avenue, Suite 300, Toronto, Ontario M4V 3B2, Canada
Penguin Books (NZ) Ltd., Cnr Rosedale & Airborne Roads, Albany, Auckland, New Zealand

First published by Penguin Books India 2001

Copyright © Uzma Aslam Khan 2001

10 9 8 7 6 5 4 3 2 1

Typeset in Sabon by Mantra Virtual Services, New Delhi

Printed at Rekha Printers Pvt. Ltd., New Delhi

For my parents

Acknowledgements

Excerpts from the Quran are taken from *Introducing the Quran to Non-Muslims and New Muslims* by A.H. Aliani (copyright held by author). I thank him for allowing me to quote his work.

Thanks also to those who helped shape this book, in particular dear Deborah, whose early faith in me was fuel for years, and my beloved Dave, who is, and will always be, my inspiration.

Part One:
A Toast

Chapter One

The carpenter Chaudry was polishing the table when Mrs Masood walked into his store. A battered radio crackled: *O Saqi! Pour me one more drink, just one more ...* He lowered the volume and bowed, 'Good morning. You're right in time. I just finished it.'

'Hmm,' she replied, spreading her fingers over the sides of the table.

'I did it all myself,' the carpenter beamed with pride. 'Exactly as you requested, with no help from the young apprentice,' he pointed to his assistant in the corner. 'How do you like it?'

From behind a curtain in the adjoining room his wife Malika quietly observed them. Tense, she cracked her toes. The customer was an old one. A few years ago she had purchased a chir cabinet from him, and many years before that her husband, who knew of Chaudry's gift for sculpting, had ordered a pair of statuettes as a wedding gift for his wife. But Chaudry had not been recompensed for either.

Some men drink blood, I ask only for wine . . .

'Oh shut it off, for heaven's sake!' the customer snapped.

The carpenter did as he was told.

Silence descended. Then Mrs Masood demanded, 'Do you have a measuring tape?'

'No, begum sahib, only my eyes.'

Mrs Masood clicked her tongue in irritation. With an imaginary tool she measured the width, murmuring, 'Five inches,' and the depth, 'Two inches,' of the border. She frowned, 'It's too wide or too narrow, too deep or too shallow. Why can't I find anything perfect these days?' Then she placed her palm over an engraved flower and squealed, 'This is as big as a real hibiscus!'

Chaudry wet his lips and nodded encouragingly. 'Notice how the weight of the flowers is balanced by the paper-thin leaves, and long delicate tendrils even finer than your hair.' When Mrs Masood flashed him a truncating look, he quickly added, 'Which is by far the finest I've ever seen.'

'Why don't you shut up?' She scowled while her fingers reached for the petals. She fondled them gingerly like a piqued child enamoured by a new toy.

The carpenter's wife, Malika, pulled a strand of her hair, remembering she was supposed to have shampooed it today. But her secret solution had finished, and she had no time to make more. No, but she must find the time, for Chaudry loved to nuzzle in her tresses when they were freshly washed. He would lift the ends and lightly shake them, 'So they can breathe,' he would say, soaking the aroma with his skin. He longed to know the ingredients of her mixture so he could wear it in a pouch

4

around his neck but she preferred to keep it hidden. Instead, she performed tricks with her uniquely supple body. His favourites were the simple ones, like piling one toe over the other to create a staircase, with the little toe perched on top like a prize. Or sliding her tongue into each nostril.

But there was one manoeuvre Chaudry begged her to forgo, though in vain, for like a bad habit she fell into it involuntarily: when enraged she flipped her feet backwards. He feared one day it would cause her to be mistaken for a witch and tried his best to keep her happy. He prayed the world would be kind to her too.

Malika was smiling at his love for her, resolving to make the shampoo later today, when Mrs Masood interrupted her reverie. 'You haven't used the wood I told you to.'

Chaudry's mouth fell open, 'But this is one hundred per cent sandalwood. Don't you smell it? You won't find anything purer in any shop in the city. Only I use it and that's because I'm an honest man, begum sahib.'

'All lies,' she waved her hand dismissively. 'And so you won't cheat me again, I'm going to pay less.'

Like the tail of a cat provoked, Malika's feet began to writhe.

The drape covering the doorway to the street was suddenly thrust aside, pulling off one of the nails that held it. A young woman dressed in a white dhoti shalwar and short, starched kameez, head and shoulders wrapped in an elaborately embroidered dupatta, stormed over the threshold. 'You said it would only take a few minutes, mummy. I've been waiting in the car for hours! Can't you hurry?'

'I'm so sorry, jaani.' Mrs Masood kissed her daughter and touched her cheek. 'You're burning! You're ill! Your complexion is ruined!' Her eyes narrowed menacingly as she screamed at Chaudry, 'This poor girl's as black as you are. And just before the wedding! I'll give you no more than one thousand rupees.'

'One thousand rupees?' Chaudry repeated. 'But when you ordered the table I said three thousand, and that too after a discount. It's worth at least four thousand, you can ask . . .'

'That's enough. You're lucky I'm buying it at all.' She unzipped her handbag, saying over her shoulders, 'Laila jaani, go tell the driver to carry this out. Then we'll leave.'

'Oh mummy, it's fabulous!' Laila shrieked, her eyes falling on the table for the first time.

Mrs Masood shook her head beckoningly at Laila, who ignored her and continued to gush. Quickly, the mother switched to speaking in English.

Malika strained but could not decipher a word. Even the woman's physical features spoke little. The smooth, fair fingers and enormous eyes, heavily coated with eyeliner, were as remote as the speech issuing from her plump, red lips.

She focused instead on Laila, who lifted her dupatta from off her head and brushed it over the table in a practised movement, inhaling blissfully. As the girl twirled through the store like a movie star, Malika approvingly noted that Chaudry modestly lowered his eyes.

Mrs Masood's tone grew brusque. But the girl threw her arms around her and surprisingly, Mrs Masood's unfathomable eyes yielded. They reminded Malika of a moth she once saw emerge fresh from its hard, wet case. The memory darkened as she remembered the moth had crumbled to earth, singed by her hot breath.

She once more embraced her daughter, as though to seal a promise. The latter clapped her hands and left the store, her dupatta trailing behind her. The mother took ten crisp one-hundred rupee notes out of her wallet and dropped them beside Chaudry. She cleared her throat and returned to speaking in Urdu. 'I'm truly disappointed in you. I so badly wanted a perfect table.' She took a deep breath and held her head in dismay. 'But something tells me not to give up on you yet. So I'm going to order another item. A bed.'

'A bed?' Chaudry gaped.

'Yes, my daughter's marital bed.' Mrs Masood's tone was keen and persuasive; Malika understood from where her daughter's acting skills originated.

'I'm sorry, begum sahib, I can't make you a bed. It's too much work for an old man like me.' He once again lowered his eyes.

'Oh but you must, you must,' she begged. 'You absolutely must.'

'I would hate to disappoint you again, and this time I myself cannot guarantee the quality of my work. For your own sake, why not try another carpenter? I know a robust one just down the road there . . . '

'Anything, I'll pay anything!'

Chaudry shook his head.

'Ten thousand? Fifteen?'

'I'm sorry, begum sahib.'

Mrs Masood's driver entered the shop. Without greeting Chaudry, he balanced the table over his shoulders saying, 'Your daughter reminds you she's waiting in the car.' Then he left, knocking a table leg against the wall.

Chaudry called after him, 'Slowly. Gently.'

'I'll give you till Christmas Eve.' Noticing Chaudry's confusion she elucidated, 'The day before our Quaid's birthday.'

Satisfied he now understood the date, she continued, 'And twenty thousand rupees.' Thus the debate ended. On her way out, Mrs Masood turned and smiled warmly, 'You choose the design. I trust you.'

As always, she left no deposit.

Behind the curtain Malika remained deathly still. She was conscious of nothing, not even the spasmodic movements of her feet. The picture of Mrs Masood beaming triumphantly, framed by the doorway to the street into which she had disappeared, an acquitted thief, had bewitched her.

Moments later, when the apprentice Talpur sat beside Chaudry and offered him tea, her mind cleared. Then her anger turned against her husband staring dumbfounded at the rupees beside him. Tomorrow, she fumed, he would forget his disappointment, and begin a new project for the very same woman who had caused it. He would spend the next two weeks impatiently waiting for the lumber to arrive, then work feverishly till the work was done, marvel at his success, and finally, once more bemoan his loss, without ever acknowledging the loss was not his alone.

For she had silently been hoping to finance their son Momin's schooling with the sale of the table. She knew she would have to do it secretly; Chaudry was opposed to his education. It would have been easy enough, as it was she who managed their accounts.

But Chaudry had failed her, as he always did whenever a Masood came to the store.

The vision of the perfectly groomed, moth-eyed customer smiling on the threshold returned to her. But this time it was not into the sunny street that she was turning, it was into the dark factory where Momin worked. It was not the resounding

8

freedom of cars that was heard but the slow, painstaking wheels of bondage. No playful wind rustled the trees and cooled the sweat off pedestrians, but instead the dark room hung still as a bat, and stank as if the creature were dead. It was into this pit that Malika now envisioned Mrs Masood falling. A tiny seat had been left empty for her on the splintered bench crammed with children, of whom Momin was one. His sparrow-sized hands were swollen abnormally from cuts that could never heal, and as he watched the lady sit beside him, he gouged a raw wound against the warp and bled on her well-preserved skin.

She turned toward the kitchen and noisily prepared to leave for the widower Mr Saeed's mansion, where she worked as a maid. On her way out, she sped past Chaudry in the store, without a word. The drape flapped in the doorway on one nail, mimicking her helplessness.

Chapter Two

The Masood family lived in a part of Karachi where residents named their houses. On the eastern side of their street was a squat cement house with a sign that read 'The Domain'. It was seldom noticed. This was followed by an enormous concoction with glazed tile towers extending at least twenty feet over the fifteen-foot wall topped with razor wire. From inside came the sound of furious barking, and every now and then a pink nose appeared briefly. This was 'Glen Castle'. Though every passer-by thought the name obscure, none publicly questioned it. Next to it was a brick house crawling with ivy called 'The Bees'. Then came a large empty plot and finally 'The Masood Paradise', a flat building with a long driveway, clipped lawns, and sprinklers playing in unison. French windows opened onto the driveway, revealing the elaborate living room where now, facing a gold-coloured divan, stood a brand new table.

Mrs Masood sat on the divan sipping an icy lemonade. She

consulted her watch, five o'clock, set the glass on a mother-of-pearl coaster on the table, and arranged her starched dupatta over her bun so it covered half her head, the nape of her neck, and most of her shoulders. Now she wanted another sip of her drink but restrained herself as the dupatta might shift. Only her eyes moved. They scanned the embossed pink and silver wallpaper, the Italian painting of a buxom virgin in an off-the-shoulder dress, the weighty velvet couch beneath it, the pink machine-made wall-to-wall carpet, and the hand-knotted burgundy one on top, with the statuettes of desert nomads sinking into its lush depths as though it were sand.

One figurine was a man, the other a woman. Both were hunched in walking position, topless. He held a walking stick in one hand and a snake in the other. She carried a baby and a pail. Loincloths covered their genitals. Mrs Masood's gaze lingered on the woman's pendulous breasts and the baby's eager mouth an inch from her nipple. Their eyes looked ahead, Mrs Masood knew, toward the edge of the desert where the well water was sweet.

Mr Masood had presented her the statuettes when he brought her to the city from Cholistan, announcing she was no longer Hinna but Mrs Masood. The statuettes were meant to represent all she had left behind. She had hated them instantly. Their dark sheesham bodies had been shaped by the carpenter Chaudry into something old and coarse, imbued with wrinkles, nudity and purpose, all of which made her shudder. Though attired differently from the people whom she had left behind, there was an inexplicable resemblance to them. Instead of reminding her of the past, they continued to be a part of her present.

She contemplated with disgust how a genius like the

carpenter's could create such ugly objects, and saw in the figurines her ageless grandmother, atop the camel Sirkash, watching her granddaughter leave the desert forever. As a bride she had not turned around to see what expression the jockey wore, for she was trying to efface the woman's creased, defiant face from her eyes. Yet she had seen it every day in the Masood Paradise—in the statuettes, the buxom Italian virgin on the wall, the reflections in the French windows, the halls, closets, even in mere emptiness—and heard her voice, ruthless as the desert wind, warning Mrs Masood to always please her husband.

She sighed and said out loud, 'This I have done. For what woman has cared for her husband and child the way I have? Which wife has better taste? Keeps a better house? And is so well rewarded?' She gazed up at the pink ceiling, where she imagined God to be, and washed her face with dry hands in a sign of respect. She thanked Him for bringing her to the city. Here life was secure and plentiful, unlike her impoverished, nomadic youth in the desert, dominated solely by the rains. Here there was an endless stream of water, and her thirst was insatiable.

While she prayed the dupatta slid down her back. 'Badmash,' she cursed. When it was satisfactorily readjusted, she pressed the plush carpet with her bare toes. It gave like a piano pedal. Her head rocked very slightly, and images floated blithely by, such as the one of Mr Masood serving red wine to his oenophile friends. She had never dared taste it, but each time he uncorked a bottle hard, obdurate vapours rushed into her with such impregnating force she felt dizzy, and alone. Yet now, as she pushed into the juicy depths of warm lambs' wool, her body imploded with myriad different sensations—confidence, serenity, vigour—all of which were sweet, sweeter than the wine denied her. This living room was her wine. She could sit here and sip it all day.

She rubbed the carpet's silken tassels with her instep and reflected on her husband's many achievements. A retired bank manager, he had established a thriving carpet business that had sent many tongues wagging: where did he get the capital? But she dismissed the gossip, even took pleasure in it. Their envy left a pleasant aftertaste.

He would be home at five thirty, only minutes from now. At the risk of once more disturbing her dupatta, she leaned forward and caressed the sandalwood table, imbibing its musky fragrance, more potent than any wine. She understood why her husband's guests chuckled after a glass or two. The scent was so intoxicating that she burst out, 'One thousand rupees!'

Mr Masood walked into the room.

'Salaam, baba,' she smiled delicately.

He was a large man with a fuzzy salt-and-pepper moustache, heavy sideburns, and hair that could not be groomed with even a dog's wide-toothed comb. It had to be thinned weekly or it shed. He nodded in response to his wife, and raised a three-dimensional eyebrow. 'I've invited the Chauclets for dinner next Thursday. The menu should be French. Ronald is bringing a friend so there'll be three. I'll instruct the cook on dessert myself. You'll see to the rest?'

Mrs Masood remained in exactly the same position. Only her smile grew to indicate affirmation. She was anticipating his approval of her new purchase. But instead he strode down the corridor, and she was left admiring it alone. Affronted, she dreamed her shaggy spouse was a cuddly sheepdog, herding her his lamb, so she could yield and gain his sanction.

As her fingertips lightly brushed the table she grew rejuvenated and gradually forgot her pain, even disregarding the dupatta rolling down her spine again. What did it matter if Mr Masood could not give affection when he had bestowed a palace? She slumped happily into the divan, her toes pushing into the carpet, forcing it to give.

Chapter Three

On the number fifteen minibus bodies hammered bodies in a desperate attempt to claim their own space. While one responded by crouching into a nondescript ball, another rose like a tornado. Malika thought, how pliable we are! Though she and Chaudry had never taken a bus together, she knew he would be the passenger who lowered his eyes, and crumpled in a corner to make room for everyone else.

Yet, she reflected, as a father he accommodated no one. At least, not as a father of sons. For Momin he had one goal: to keep him off the streets, where his older brothers had failed. He employed one method: work. Shauqat and Moeez had failed because they were not made to work enough. Malika pleaded to have young Momin sent to school, but Chaudry insisted, 'The discipline our boy accumulates will serve him till death, for skill is greater than education.' He would say this while hacking dead wood, blowing splinters off its surface, smoothening edges adeptly with sandpaper, and stepping back to admire the emerging product.

In actuality Momin brought home more than Chaudry's version of discipline. His daily wages of six rupees were stocked away for the baby girl's dowry. But the life he led was perhaps no less perilous than a life on the streets, for by the age of five he had inhaled so much fibre at the factory that Malika could pluck it from the air he exhaled. While he slept, she would listen to his body and hear the devil beating it like a sheet of tin. She would cover his eyes with tealeaves, coaxing the blue gossamer lids to cease fluttering, and wonder what visions disturbed the six hours of rest he was permitted. Nightly, she soothed his tumid fingers, dyed orange with henna to cool the sores, and turned to the other bed where Chaudry snored contentedly after a fruitless day at work.

The air in the bus was so thick passengers were jostled into numbness. Their supple faces flopped loosely on thread-thin necks. When the bus braked, their heads rolled back, then forward again. Some men kept alert by grinning lecherously at the few women on board. Others pawed them. Malika hardened against their touch, and bitterly reflected that Chaudry would forever remain hardened against Momin's.

It was all up to her then.

She had been promising Momin for a year that she would rescue him from the loom, and offer instead a classroom. It would be just between them, she had hugged him, hoping that by sharing her dream she could gain his trust. But when Chaudry's every contract ended in a loss, she feared her son, with his five-year-old's intuition, had stopped believing in her. At home he had developed the habit of settling quietly in a corner like an abandoned pup. This time, however, she would do whatever it took to keep her promise.

Her thoughts turned to the older boys, Shauqat and Moeez. Eventually, perhaps, she could get them back too.

She had seen the latter's ruddy cheeks turn grey, the rims of his eyes resemble pomegranate pulp, the loss of his rewarding appetite, and worse, of his smile. She had noticed too that Shauqat seemed to gain the pounds Moeez was shedding, and that Moeez's many friends who lurked outside their house asked instead for Shauqat. But she had not known what it would lead to—Moeez's theft, nearly four years ago, of all their savings. Unfortunately it was Chaudry, not she, who made the discovery and she had had no choice but to watch while the fine-boned, shrivelled man belted the skin off her once-robust son's back. He would have whipped him to death had Malika not brought the neighbours. When they held him back and Moeez lay doubled on the floor, vomiting blood, he confessed to being in Shauqat's debt for heroin.

Chaudry threw them both out of the house and turned his back on them forever. He resolved that Momin, who was then not even old enough to say 'Aba', would be like him or no one else. Three years later they had a daughter. With her, fatherhood became sheer, unadulterated happiness, while motherhood suddenly turned barren.

She looked out of the grimy windows. People hung over the railings of their balconies, watching the traffic roll down the street. Occasionally, someone shuffled into one of the pistachio-coloured apartments, and it was hard to know if it was the same person that later returned.

A few banners bearing the dupatta-framed face of the recently ousted Prime Minister remained. They billowed beside the face of the caretaker Prime Minister. A few feet ahead, there were others of the opposition leader most likely to come into power. All left her indifferent. What did it matter if the country was led by a general or a woman? She still had to ride the bus, strike or not, war in Afghanistan or peace in India. Her boys were still lost, her husband was still cheated, and she still had to find a way to enroll Momin in school. Let those faces flap in the wind.

More important to her were the scavenger kites perched on rooftops and billboards. Momin adored them. He had revealed his love of birds to her last winter, while they gazed wondrously at the scores of migratory herons flying over the city to Haleji Lake. She had told him of the flamingoes of Kutch that built nests of mud on the salt flats with their great jaws. 'They tilt their heads so the upper jaw becomes the lower one and that's the one that moves.'

Astounded, Momin had clasped his mouth and felt, for the first time in his minor life, the slack hinges of his lower jaw. 'It's loose,' she had smiled, flipping her head like the great pink bird and pretending to feed like it.

The landscape beyond the greasy windows was swiftly altering from congested streets flanked by drab apartment complexes to capacious boulevards flanked by coconut trees. The bus halted near the angular facade of the KMC Sports Complex. Malika pushed aside the clawing and dawdling alike, one of whom caressed her throat then yanked off her dupatta. While retrieving it, she stepped on a big toe swollen past the size of the heel, with a loose flap of red skin hanging in place of the nail. Flies hovering over it followed her off the bus. Her heart sank: the toe was a foreshadowing of what Momin's hands would become unless she acted fast.

With heavy footsteps, she headed for the old ancestral home

18

of Mr Saeed and his hopelessly anglicized, motherless children. She turned into a side street distinguished by a blue-tiled mosque with rows of Peshawari slippers splattered on its steps, and in the distance located the white marble floor of Mr Saeed's balcony, spotted with rotten mangoes and pomegranates. There loomed his gaunt, towering frame in a tattered silk dressing gown. It would be pointless waving. He would not notice.

Since the death of his wife, Mr Saeed devoted himself to the making of a museum where he buried his nose in Art. When he had hired Malika it was as a cleaning woman, cook and, above all else, mother. 'Be easy with them,' he had said, inebriated with sorrow, vanishing into the not-so-distant past of his colonial relics. He did not like her cleaning his study so she had not seen much of him since then. But when scrubbing the rest of the house details of him followed her: the thin, dry lips; grey, sunken cheeks; brooding brow. There were no bright lights in his burrow for he wanted always to live in shadow, but even fire could not give lustre to those features.

She reached the heavy iron gate, rapped on it, and mused on how alike he and her husband were. While one collected, the other created, each with a fever that enfeebled him in the world. Mr Saeed was unaware that his eldest child religiously failed her classes, that his ten-year-old son still wet his bed, or that the seven-year-old only drank from a bottle. And Chaudry remained oblivious to little Momin, who had ceased growing at five and sighed in his sleep like a dead man turning in his grave.

An old, half-blind doorman, who was occasionally also the gardener, shuffled to let her in. 'Thank you, baba,' Malika smiled. They walked in silence up the sweeping driveway, he dangling an enormous ring with rusting keys. At the front door he fumbled for one that miraculously worked. 'Thank you, baba,' she repeated, and entered the wood-panelled, termite-infested living room. This was smothered with photographs of Mr Saeed's grandfather, a lean bearded man with jocular eyes, and his majestic Arab horses. In others, the polo-adoring English viceroy, Lord Mountbatten, sat atop a glistening black mare, and Lady Mountbatten in a light summer dress waved as she entered a long, bumblebee-shaped vehicle whose doors were propped open by a waistcoated man in a tall turban. There were no photographs of the dead Mrs Saeed.

After the downstairs was swept and dusted, she held her breath and mounted the tortuously narrow staircase with steps that spiralled at absurdly sharp angles. The climb required elf-like grace, or else tiny feet, neither of which Malika possessed. She often wondered which of the two qualities Mr Saeed's princely forefathers had been blessed with, probably the former, for his children were not petite, yet they raced up the staircase with impossible ease. But perhaps their mother, had she not met her death falling off a horse, might well have found it here.

The rooms on the first floor were the children's. Their bedrooms were large, with windows overlooking the abandoned stables at the back of the house. Malika sprayed cleaner on the glass, and while wiping, looked down at the stalls where once horses glistened and brayed. After lunch, the children would sometimes pull her there to play with the ghosts of these animals. Or they would lead her to the ruins of the amphitheatre beside the stables, carrying sheets beneath which they shrieked 'housie', the word curiously echoing impotence. Their father's balcony hung above the arena's broken steps but he never once emerged.

His absence had turned the eldest child Saima into a tempest. Malika smoothed the sheets of her bed, wondering what mood the girl would be in today. If gay, she would return from school with amusing tales of the English principal Mr Brown's lily-white children, and mimic their tight-lipped speech. If sour, she would talk of teachers who belittled her in front of the class. They sent her to the principal, who lectured her on low grades, though she knew of others who had worse. Her favourite place for spilling frustration was at her father's closed door. 'When that mouse comes out of his hole, tell him the principal's dying to make his *treasured* acquaintance!' Or, 'When that egghead hatches, tell him Mr Brown's waiting for the yolk! Maybe then he'll get off my bloody back! Everyone else's father has him nicely fattened!'

Her second favourite outlet was Malika. She mocked her illiteracy, 'Read me a story!' She glared at her feet and screamed, 'Ooh, watch them twist! The devil made you, churail!' And frequently, Saima accused her of not cleaning properly, stealing or eating too much. But one happy outcome of Saima's anger was that eventually it led her to the many books spread around the room. She would read to herself then, sometimes even to her brothers, and Malika did not have to listen to her prattle or rave.

Fazeel, the second, was easiest to contend with. A shy boy, he was happiest when ignored. Though only ten, he had a room to himself. After a speedily devoured lunch, he clambered up to it, and spent the afternoon playing with soldiers and planes till Malika insisted he sleep. Then he answered to the air: 'All right, stupid.'

Faisal, the youngest, shared Saima's room. She dressed him for school every morning, washed and fed him, slapped and squeezed him till he all but popped. In the afternoons, when Malika was with them, the seven-year-old clung to her the most. He whimpered and insisted on drinking from a bottle.

The house had four floors and a terrace at the top. The second floor was Mr Saeed's and the third had belonged to his wife. Sometimes, when Mr Saeed grew tired of his balcony, he would mount to the terrace, and from downstairs she could see him, more shadowy than ever before. Everything above the first floor was off-limits to Malika, which made her work easier.

After the children's rooms were tidied, she paused at the landing to recite a lengthy prayer, for she especially feared the descent. On the last step, she sighed with relief. The kitchen was left to mop, the table to arrange, and then it was time to make lunch.

Finally, she settled behind Mr Saeed's driver in the old, low-slung Mercedes to fetch his children from school. She sat close to the door, for though this had been her afternoon routine for several years now, after a lifetime on the bus she could not grow accustomed to having the entire back seat to herself. She gazed out of the windows—no less grimy than a bus's—and anticipated how happy the children would be to see her.

In the mid-afternoon, as they dozed restfully in their air-conditioned rooms, over soft mattresses and beneath plush covers that Malika herself had replaced, she counted another day without Momin.

Chapter Four

From the French windows in the living room, Mrs Masood surveyed Mr Afraz in the paradise of the Masood Paradise. He was the highly recommended topiary specialist hired to please the diplomat M. Chauclet, an important asset to the French Ministry of Commerce and Industry, and Laila's future father-in-law.

He and Mr Masood had met on a government-sponsored trip to promote rapidly dwindling carpet imports by France. Mr Masood had taken his daughter with him, hoping her acting skills would help to elicit compassion. Together, father and daughter had described how ignominious the embargo was, based on absurd charges, for the carpets were made by children whose families depended on them for their livelihood, who freely chose to work, indeed, for Tradition. Thus child-labour propaganda, they argued, was 'false and baseless', and actually hurt the very children it claimed to protect, crippling the nation's economy, forcing the government to subsidize twenty-five per cent of the industry. Carpet manufacturers were establishing welfare centres to ensure the children were well paid, and their health in tiptop condition.

M. Chauclet had seen the injustice, and promised to help the Government of Pakistan, represented by the philanthropic Masoods.

His son, thus far unsuccessful with women, was delighted when his flirtatious overtures toward Laila were met with batting lashes. And his family was delighted when their feeble son at last captured *something*.

The wedding was to be on New Year's Day but the ceremonies would commence on Christmas Eve. In M. Chauclet's honour, shrubs in the shape of reindeer, sledges and even Santa Claus were to be transplanted, surrounded by smaller ones sculpted into typical Christmas ornaments, like angels, which would then be decorated with the actual ornament itself.

The idea had been inspired by a picture of Versailles Mrs Masood had seen in a book called *All The World Loves France*. The neatly shaven trees in adroitly delineated rows were unlike anything her desert-weary eyes had ever seen. She ordered a wall-to-wall print of the gardens for her living room and suggested to her husband that they duplicate the shrubs in their garden but choose the designs to suit the season. *Et voila*! She had found the perfect melange, to which even her impassive husband gave his compliments. She had spent the next few days imagining he were Louis XIV, and she his queen.

The gardeners were pulling out the pink champa, anthurium and asphodels that had been planted years before by a landscape artist attempting a typical English layout. But Mrs Masood had never been satisfied with the design, and was now especially pleased to see the wild purple flowers, as dense as Mr Masood's hair, thrust into a heap of torn bushes. She turned and magnificently strode into another area of her palace: the kitchen.

Tonight the Chauclets were coming to dinner. Waiters from the Sheraton Hotel had been hired to serve them. Her own servants, although hard working, were not publicly presentable. They either stammered, or were fat, coal-complexioned and flat-footed, or simply smiled too much.

The cook Tufail was teaching his assistant Jamil how to debone pomfret when Mrs Masood entered. Her eyes instantly fell on the imported wine-red raspberries on the counter. Next to them stood a 750 ml bottle of Grand Marnier for the sauce. The bottle was sealed but her husband would never know if she opened it and took a sniff. She gazed at its long neck and convex body, the frosted glass and antique label, and longed to discover how the vapours would tease her.

Tufail and Jamil were patting the fish with breadcrumbs and were aeons away from guessing her intentions. Her heart raced. All of a sudden she was an impostor in her own palace and would have to act quickly, and ever so stealthily, or be hanged! She was the fox in a chicken coop, the child in an adult theatre, Rushdie in Khomeini's bed. Snap! What if the crack of the seal was heard as far away as Mr Masood's office? She raised the bottle tremulously to her nose.

Just then Jamil's twin Khalil barged into the kitchen. Startled, Mrs Masood dropped the bottle. The liquor spilled like a loosened chignon, running over the floor and under cabinets.

'Get it, you fools!' she screamed.

Though most of its contents were lost, the bottle remained intact. Khalil wiped its exterior with a sponge while Jamil mopped the floor and Tufail reached under the stove for the rolling cap.

'God help me!' Mrs Masood gasped at the orange puddle at her feet.

'D-d-don't worry, mad-dam,' assured Tufail. 'The recipe calls only for ab-b-bout what's left.'

'But if they want to drink it? How will I explain? Oh, it's all your fault!' She grabbed Khalil by his kurta collar and boxed his ear.

Jamil, the older of the two by seconds, interceded, 'Forgive him, baji.'

'Devil!' Mrs Masood turned on Jamil.

'Let me explain, baji,' Khalil pleaded. 'There's a thirsty masi outside . . . '

'There's no masi or wasi there, you liars,' Mrs Masood slapped them in succession. They raised their arms in defence. 'You're both dismissed!' They waited but as she was inexorable, they bolted out of the kitchen. She was left with Tufail who eyed her suspiciously. 'Get back to work,' she commanded.

Soon the kitchen looked as it had before the accident. Although bubbles of soap still lingered in their crevices, the floor tiles were dry. The counter and bottle were spotless. Mrs Masood noticed a thick, fruity essence around her. Was it the Grand Marnier? She sniffed. A strange combination of citrus, bleach, fish and onions charged into her head. She left the kitchen feeling nauseated and aware that her dupatta was ruffled from the tussle with the twins. 'Damn them!'

Outside, Malika hovered powerlessly over the twins.

'Look what you've done,' Khalil sobbed, smearing his cheeks with dirty hands. 'We're fired.'

'But I don't understand.' She fretfully drew near. 'Why?'

'Go away,' the boy wept loudly now.

'Don't be a girl,' Jamil scoffed. 'I'll tell you what happened,' he turned on Malika. 'When Khalil ran inside to get you water, he alarmed the begum and she dropped something so important it made her crazy.' Eyeing her menacingly, he pulled a pack of K2 from his kurta pocket and struck a match with practised aggression. Slowly, he sucked in the first drag. 'That's what comes of helping people.' He flicked ash first her way, then at his twin.

'She said she was thirsty!' Khalil confusedly defended Malika's honour to save his own.

'She?' Jalil pretended to choke. 'Camels don't need water, you fool!'

Malika shuddered at the hatred in his voice but once more offered an apology, adding, 'Maybe I can explain to her that it was all an unfortunate misunderstanding, perhaps when she's calmer?'

Jamil threw his head back and laughed a long, humourless laugh. It echoed in her mind long after he grew silent. She shook her head, certain that in coming here she had committed the kind of error that would only snowball.

She could not explain, even to herself, why she had hopped onto a different bus that afternoon. It was a Thursday, the end of the week, the day she treated Mr Saeed's children to an outing. They had piled into the old Mercedes and she had directed the driver to their favourite destination—Empress Market. For all three of them, a day at the dirty, noisy bazaar was as promising as a circus. Faisal was delighted with the curly pink prawns. He picked one up, expecting it to writhe like a worm. When it hung still, he twirled it, then shrieked for added effect. Malika herself drew no pleasure from these 'treats'. There was nothing wondrous about the slimy piles of blue lobster with protruding black eyes daring her to pluck them, and nothing sensational about the raucous parrots shrieking in fecal prisons, 'I can talk!' The slobbering, brown puppies for sale were part of her routine landscape, like the goats lined up for slaughter. But, she thought, if her own son sought these very diversions, she would perhaps view them differently.

An idea, vague yet urgent, had crept into her brain. If she could get into the house of the factory-owner Mr Masood and his wretched wife who stole from them, somehow, she would be closer to her son. So after work, she waved on the number fifteen minibus and rode the eight, asking for directions along her walk.

Outside the kitchen, Jamil watched her sardonically, challenging her to break the ice. She resolved not to be intimidated, and turned her attention instead to the kinder twin. Like his brother, Khalil had an athletic physique, smooth tawny skin, and beautiful luminous eyes. But it was easy to tell them apart. Jamil was taller, leaner and confronted the world with an arched brow, as though the inch he had over his brother diminished everyone. Khalil, who had stopped weeping and gazed absently at the air, wore a looser, friendlier expression. His lashes were moist with tears and in the sunlight they shimmered like gems. She felt a tenderness for him. He was like her second son Moeez, immured by Shauqat, who had an uncanny resemblance to Jalil.

'Where are you from, son?' she gently addressed Khalil.

Disappointment obscured his sapphire eyes. She had failed him, just as she had Moeez, and just as she now failed Momin. He gazed at her despairingly then shuffled to the servants' quarters around the back of the house.

She was left with Jamil. He studied her with artificial

calmness: head cocked, fingers lightly picking tobacco from his tongue.

She quietly strode down the driveway, disconcerted by the mirror image of Shauqat, anticipating the fate of the weaker twin. It occurred to her that she had not accomplished her goal of entering the house.

Gardeners thoughtlessly tossed delicate purple flowers her way. She paused, wondering at the mess. Picking up a discarded bunch, she headed for the road again. The drooping, weeping bouquet reminded her of the light extinguished from the dazzling eyes of Khalil. She chucked the flowers in a gutter as she reached the road, muttering, 'Why should I care about them?' The seraph and his devil-brother had been expelled from the Masood Paradise. There was no reason why she should not replace them.

Chapter Five

There were six seated at the table—the three Masoods, two Chauclets, and a M. Didier. The latter had travelled to Pakistan, on the recommendation of M. Chauclet, to investigate opening an outlet of Mr Masood's products in France. It was the first offer for international expansion Mr Masood had ever received. He had given his wife firm instructions to keep M. Didier happy. She was failing. The latter expressed bitter disappointment as course after course turned out to be French instead of Pakistani.

'But you must recognize the gracious hostess' intention, Paul, is to make us feel at home,' M. Chauclet gently interceded.

'But we aren't at home, that's the point!' M. Didier was a tall man whose muscular shoulders entirely concealed his neck, giving him the demeanour of a vulture perpetually on the verge of attack.

He had none of the friendly twinkle of the Director of the Cabinet of Exterior Commerce, Laila's future father-in-law, a round, balding man who sipped his vichyssoise and winked at Mrs Masood. 'Don't mind Paul, Madame!'

Still, the vulture persisted, 'What do you normally eat?' With his spoon he indicated the uniformed servers, 'Ask them to bring me some of it.'

Though seated at opposite ends of the table, Mr and Mrs Masood winced as one. Nervously, the wife cleared her throat. 'What we eat varies. Our cook knows dishes from all over the world.'

'Then where is he?' M. Didier waved his spoon excitedly. 'Why don't I see him?'

Reluctantly, Mrs Masood asked a server to call Tufail, the pockmarked cook she had hoped to conceal.

When he appeared, M. Didier asked, 'Is it true you make dishes from around the world?'

The cook looked questioningly at Mrs Masood. She nimbly translated the Frenchman's mucous English into Urdu. Tufail nodded.

'Excellent,' M. Didier replied. 'Then make me something you would eat.'

M. Chauclet interrupted, 'Paul, surely you can't expect this poor man to cook from scratch, he's worked hard enough. Maybe you could sample some leftovers.' He turned to Mrs Masood, 'I'm sure there's something native tucked away in the refrigerator?'

'An excellent idea!' M. Didier raised his wineglass, first to Tufail, then to Mrs Masood.

A stuffy odour, similar to ammonia, steeped her lungs and irritated her senses. There were plenty of *native* dishes *tucked away*, but why should they want those when she had spent days planning this menu? No one had uttered a word of praise for her

31

work and how dare that carrion-picker toast Tufail and herself in the same sweep of an arm! 'Go heat up the mutton korma,' she snapped at Tufail.

'K-k-korma . . . ?'

'Hurry!'

Perplexed, the cook shuffled away.

The financial prospects of a French-Pakistani carpet venture soon shimmered Mrs Masood into allegiance. She smiled beneficently at the prospective buyer, swooping shoulders, beady eyes, wrinkled beak and all. 'It will only take a moment.' She stole another glance at Mr Masood for his sheepdog approval of her flawless tact. Inert to feminine charm, he lifted the fragile stem of his wineglass and lightly turned it. She thought it a gesture entirely ill suited to hands as clumsy as his.

To her left sat the young lovers. Laila, in a pale lilac dress that fell in lush, tantalizing folds all the way to her feet, was drowned so blissfully in courtship that her mother guessed she had missed the entire episode with M. Didier. She sat still with flushed cheeks, her sloe eyes fixed on the young Chauclet, André. The boy too burned with an ecstasy exclusively his own. Absently, he brushed with manicured fingers the downy hair falling gently on his white forehead. Or scratched a love-enflamed nostril of his bony nose.

He was as effeminate as Mr Masood was sloppy; neither was handsome. But, mused Mrs Masood, André would make Laila happy. She would settle in the succulent French countryside and be even happier than her mother, for André would not only shower Laila with wealth, but also with utmost devotion. Mrs Masood sighed contentedly as the boy twitched his nose and a rosy hue spread across his pallid cheeks. What mother would not want her daughter married to a boy of his status? Once more she would have the envy of all of Pakistan.

Tufail entered with a steaming plate of curry.

'Bravo!' M. Didier declared, and M. Chauclet and Mr Masood echoed him as he raised a toast: 'To the native leftovers in the refrigerator.' Rapaciously, they sucked their drinks and tore the meat.

Mrs Masood followed the last trickle of wine as it slid along the curved side of her husband's glass, marking the maroon colour thin to a pinker shade till only very faint dots remained, like the bloody spots in her armpits after a fresh waxing. He licked the spots, probing into the bowl till the rim obstructed his lump of a nose and his tongue could delve no further. Then he poured himself another glass.

The acid fumes that earlier vexed her transformed into a new sensation, soft and mellow like rosewater. A surge of sweet nostalgia overcame her as she thought of her grandmother in the shifting sands of Cholistan.

But, like a drunkard who tries to keep a clear head, she urgently shook herself, realizing that what she experienced was mere nostalgia for nostalgia. She suddenly felt hopelessly barren. Her past was a graveyard.

Mr Masood offered more wine to M. Didier, who was guzzling his with increasing speed. His forehead grew sweaty. He wiped it in long, hurried strokes that messed his hair and gave him the appearance of a perturbed predator who senses his feathers are ruffled but cannot see them. Mrs Masood was almost touched to find the beast baffled. She envied his silliness, and longed for the carefree camaraderie of all the men as they lapsed into inebriety. The wine that splashed gregariously up the sides of their cherub-cheeked glasses, a drop or two falling heedlessly on the new lace tablecloth, cruelly mocked her solitude. As she helped herself to a Normandy crêpe daintily topped with a sprig of parsley, she imagined washing it down with a sip of the men's wine. She would relish it better than they, by twirling her glass with poise and long fingers. But the dry crêpe scratched her throat, forcing her to abandon the fantasy and pay attention to reality: the men making merry at one end, and the lovers excruciatingly private love at the other.

André had drawn closer to his betrothed. He whispered in her ear, just to brush against her tight, silken cheeks. He lingered longer than Mr Masood would have permitted. But despite their obliviousness to the outer world, the lovers were acutely aware that the patriarch was happily preoccupied. André's mouth hovered around Laila's like a bee drifting over a flower, gauging the best place to settle. Her plump, uninitiated mouth, it occurred to Mrs Masood, would soon taste the air of a foreign land. Perhaps the air of a vineyard, thick with fruit and flies. What juices would perfume those red lips? Would it be wine? Would a wet cerise stain forever lacquer the sensuous curves of her daughter's mouth, the curves— inherited from her—around which the bee had finally surrendered?

Honed by solitude, Mrs Masood's thoughts returned to familiar ghosts: her aunts and grandmother. All of them had slept together—with her smothered in the centre of them like prey—on one large bed strung with garlic and onions to ward off the sah pina snakes that crept into a sleeper's breath and poisoned it. During the day these women lived hurried lives: washing, cooking, cleaning and occasionally whisking away for a few urgent moments with a spouse behind a curtain. She was noticed only when plates needed drying, potatoes peeling, or rice sieving. Her companions were the distorted images of stories the women related as they lingered over dinner, when the day's work was accomplished, and the men were satisfied.

As night drew close and the women finished their meal, a renewed hunger overcame them. Loosening their long tresses with calloused fingers, they oiled each other's heads and spoke of witches with feet turned backwards, churails who hunted innocent humans for their hearts. And djinns, invisible creatures born of the fire of desert winds, who lived as parasites on a human soul, gnawing at it with astringent jaws, leaving it raw, fringe-edged. They described in gruesome detail the agony of one victim, who sought the succour of cool water with which to soothe her burns. But every well, pool or puddle faded into the sky as she approached. Finally she found a giant-sized pool large enough to fit an entire civilization, a relic of ancient Harappa perhaps, and plunged inside. The pool was hollow.

The story Mrs Masood remembered best was one her grandmother narrated frequently. She swore that her father had carried a churail on his shoulders for weeks.

'How did she find him?' an aunt would ask.

Pleased at this chance to narrate the story, the revered matriarch would lapse into a slow narrative.

'My father and his brother were little boys living in a dusty village not unlike this one,' she would begin. 'The straw for houses, spices for curries, khaddi for cloth, wood for fire, everything between and including earth and sky was tinged yellow. The sun played such tricks even the night was gold.' She would shut her eyes to better soak the oil one of her daughters massaged vigorously into her head, for oil sharpened the mind. No one dared rush her.

Finally, she would continue, 'My father and his brother passed rows of scorched trees with leaves so dry you itched for days if they grazed you, which they did often, as they needed your moisture. Carefully they dodged the thirsty branches, their ears alert for the slightest rustle for there was no wind. The leaves should have been silent. Sometimes, the long shiny tail of a skink dangled before their eyes, its smooth scales glinting with sunlight, the tail becoming a quivering, spangled lash as it reached for them. Nor were they safe in a clearing, for the sand beneath their feet shifted constantly. There were ant-tracks, snake-tracks, scorpion-tracks, porcupine-tracks, bird-tracks and human-tracks.'

Again she would pause, this time to inhale the unctuous smell of mustard oil smothering the air. To escape the garish odour, little Hinna would bury her face in a pillow. But her own head was also massaged with the oil, as were those of all the other women, so every pillow stank of it. She would pinch her nose and quickly grow light-headed as the grandmother continued, 'One day my father and his brother found tracks neither could identify. They were small, a woman's size, with five digits but shaped like claws. The boys stepped into the footprints and followed them, finding they were walking backwards.'

Each aunt drew her breath simultaneously, shaking her head. One suggested, 'If only they had been warned.' Another looked sternly into Hinna's young eyes, 'Don't ever make the same mistake!' And a chorus agreed, 'You're lucky to have us watch over you.' Woozy-eyed, the child quickly screened their feet.

The grandmother never welcomed interruptions. Proudly, she would resume, 'Backwards they walked, one behind the other, my uncle looking over his shoulder and laughing at my father who cursed him every time he tripped on him. So occupied were they in keeping on the backward track, they did not notice the ground grow damp and dark. Gone were the shifting sands, the thirsty leaves, and sun-dipped saurians. The track too had vanished. Instead, they were caught in a mesh of leaves and weed, all tangled with roots and branches that climbed high up into a black sky and dangled over them in noose-like shadows. They whispered, "Where are we?"

'A sweet voice answered, "Are you lost?" A little girl was perched on the bloated roots of an old mangrove tree. "Come," she beckoned gently. Surprisingly, the boys found themselves free to move. Darkness shed a layer of her cloak so they could follow the little girl's long braids, swinging like snares.

'They reached a small hut where she disappeared behind a door to make tea. My uncle and father curiously walked around the room. It smelled dense, not the still, humid heaviness of the forest, but different . . . '

Hinna, steeped in yellow pillows, wondered if it was mustard the poor boys had smelt. And if the churail's house reeked of mustard, as did hers . . . Again she examined the women's feet as the story continued.

'The odour was strongest along the walls lined with tables and shelves with wobbly legs. On them they found bowls of blackwood. On tiptoe they peered inside, and cried "Oof!" and pinched their noses, while my father dipped his finger into the bowl. In horror he stared at the thick red fluid on his skin.'

The child breathed a sigh of relief, for the mixture was red, not yellow, and so her aunts were not witches.

'Just then the girl returned with a tea tray. Instantly, they saw her feet pointed backwards. The boys rushed out of the house but it was too late. She flew over them, now settling on my father's shoulders, now on my uncle's, all the while screeching like an owl, "You'll never get away! I'm going to eat your heart! You'll never get away!"'

The grandmother would shake her long, silvery hair and hiss at the circle like a reptile from her own story. She would order the end of the massage and the telling of another tale.

But Hinna always longed to know what had happened to the boys. If her great-grandfather grew to father her grandmother, surely he must have got rid of the witch. But how? And did his brother survive? How did her great-grandfather sleep with the witch on top of him? The evil creature must have weighed even more than the pungent mustard cloud permanently smothering her.

These and other questions haunted her as she lay tucked between her grandmother and aunts on a large charpoi, after each of them had told their unfinished tales. The westerly windows of their meagre hut were thrown open, beckoning all evil inside. She heard feet flap, felt them brush her hair, but kept her eyes shut till she feared they bled. Only this frightened her more, for it was blood the witch wanted, and her bloody eyes might attract an entire family of them. She tried to envision a calming scene, but the only pictures that appeared were from other stories, like the shrivelled woman drowning in a hollow pool. She imagined falling into the vast hole in a breathless dive that her grandmother said would last forever, explaining that this was what city folk called 'hell'.

She watched lizards scurrying on the thatched ceiling, wondering if there were good and bad ones. They landed one after the other, thump, thump, thump, smack on her mustard pillow. As a last resort, she curled into the curve of her grandmother's spine, and concentrated like a yogi on the rhythm of the old woman's steady breathing. Then, if patient, she glimpsed heaven. It appeared in those murky seconds between sleep and consciousness when her body, tense as a crystal, eventually relaxed; when heat from her grandmother's broad, rustic back melted her from ice into a river. Fearlessly, she rushed down mountains, toppling stones and gurgling a song that eventually lulled her to sleep.

She thought now, while choking down the dry crêpe, how others had always envied her for being in the care of the ancient woman, to whom they attributed supernatural powers. Yet the only time Mrs Masood had loved her was when she slept. Otherwise, the tall, vigorous woman embodied the oddities of her tales, vanishing for days to commune with the desert, where it was rumoured she lived on fern seeds. Thus, her aunts explained, she turned invisible, and saw what blinded others.

On her visible days, she regarded the child with suspicion, or dismissed her for having a scrambled brain that rendered her useless to the family. 'Bah! Just like your mother!' she would scoff, her only oblique reference to the woman Mrs Masood had never known. Her aunts gossiped: their sister-in-law had eloped ... she had been offered as compensation in a land feud ... she had died of an unknown grief. But when they knew the girl was listening, they hushed each other with knowing eyes.

Once, while she and her grandmother were taking their early morning walk to the basin to wash, she had dared to ask when she might see her mother.

Her face like cracked plaster, the old woman answered haughtily, 'Do you not see me?'

The child drew her breath, vowing never to speak of the missing link again.

But it was too late. Her grandmother was affronted, and as punishment inflicted the greatest insult of all: instead of using the cup they had brought, she bathed her body, all sixty-seven inches of it, with only a fistful of water. She urged the child to follow, then watched icily as Hinna's awkward fingers struggled with a third fistful, and then a fourth, on a frame that was less than half the dexterous grandmother's. She spat irritably, 'The desert curses you for wasting its jewel!'

The child grew to dread both her grandmother's presence, and absence, for the latter meant sleepless nights of even worse torment. But eventually, at the age of sixteen, she was granted relief. She blossomed into a pretty, fair-skinned adolescent whom the family realized could be married well. She had none of the burliness of her aunts, but resembled instead a slim mountaineer with a high forehead and Mughal nose, whom she saw only in the virile blur behind the curtain where her aunts occasionally vanished. She wondered if the smudge was her father. It was at this time that Mr Masood drew his first awestruck breath and promised her a new life.

He was living in Bahawalpur but the bank where he worked had transferred him to its new branch in Karachi. In his free time, he hunted the timid birds of Cholistan, but ended up freeing one instead. 'Come with me,' he had tossed aside the rifle, much to the dismay of his assistant, who was forced to spend the wedding festivities clearing it of sand, 'and your life will be sweeter than wine.'

Her grandmother, sensing the man's ardour, refused. When he persisted, she explained she could not afford a dowry. He agreed. She still refused. He offered her a price, doubled it, tripled it, till finally, the wily guardian gave her consent.

On the afternoon before the wedding, while Hinna was being rubbed with wheat to soften her skin, the old woman counselled her. 'Evil frequents those who defy their roles in life. Men are weak when they aim below their means, women when they aim above. My father fell prey to the churail because he

40

walked backwards. He followed a woman. But to be a good wife, you must always follow at your husband's heel, so he knows where you are.'

Mrs Masood now observed the servers while they cleared the table, placed fresh plates, and refilled glasses before dessert. Her husband and M. Chauclet slapped each other fondly on the shoulders. She prepared a smile in case they should look at her. They had ravished the korma, but the crêpes, fillet of fish, flan of foie gras in mushroom sauce and gratin of potato, all remained untouched. She wondered if, after the guests left, Mr Masood would blame her for the culinary failure or, if the alliance with M. Didier materialized, he would in fact forgive her. Most probably, he would fall asleep and never mention tonight at all. Still, her grandmother should rest assured, for she had done as he bid.

After the wedding, when he brought her to the city, Mr Masood came to realize his wife was a heavy liability. She was completely illiterate, and spoke not a word of English. Compelled by a sense of his social standing, he employed a full-time English tutor, as well as a woman to cultivate in his wife city manners and tastes that he hoped would inflict a shame of her past. She was Hinna no more. But she learned slowly, and while sleeping reverted to her native Seraiki.

When he first developed the habit of mentioning he could have married a lady of fortune instead, she felt her grandmother snuggle up to her when she slept. In the mornings, mustard breath lingered in her hair. Sometimes the blankets turned suddenly to lead, pressing her like a steaming iron. She would try to rise from the bed, to glance out at the lush gardens outside—the neat, orderly gardens that *she* controlled—but the weight paralysed her. She wondered nightly how her great-grandfather could have slept with the churail atop him and demanded of the invisible woman beside her why *she*, who did her utmost to please her husband, was being punished.

Dessert arrived, breaking Mrs Masood's reverie. M. Didier said, 'Only yesterday I had the misfortune of sampling a local dessert, something round and sticky by the name of rose something . . . ' He waved his hand under Mrs Masood's nose to incite her memory, but she was too struck by how uncomely he was to reply. He was soaked in sweat and had thrust open the top few buttons of his shirt, so that his tie was crooked. He resembled a sopping duckling whose mother had disappeared in the middle of a preening session. He frowned and continued, 'Well, I must confess it was terrible so this,' he took an enormous helping of the raspberries, 'I will gladly accept.'

Following his example, the other men smothered the red, pulpous bodies with Grand Marnier sauce, while André snaked around the porcelain slope of Laila's neck. Mrs Masood, nibbling her plain portion of fruit, solicitously sniffed the creamy, orange scent that swept across the table. The men were preoccupied with the lavishly sodden berries . . . they would never know. Did she dare taste the magical ingredient her husband had forbidden?

'Follow at his heels . . . ' she heard her grandmother's warning.

But did it mean she should do as he ordered, or that she should act exactly like him?

The guests heaped second helpings, burped and heaved full-bellied sighs. 'Superb dinner, Madame,' M. Chauclet congratulated. 'You're only too lucky to have such a cook. The sauce is particularly ingenious. Why aren't you having any?'

She nodded politely. Mr Masood answered on her behalf,

'Our women are prohibited the consumption of alcohol. It's unIslamic.'

M. Chauclet returned her smile. 'Cultural differences fascinate me. Your customs concerning women, food and,' he paused, 'labour. We must be sympathetic.'

Mr Masood grinned at the first allusion to the carpet contract that evening. Mrs Masood could hear his heart race in anticipation, and her own too raced at the prospect of another venture. She decided then that if Mr Masood's wish were granted, if he succeeded in establishing a market in France, why then, she too would fulfil her desire: *she would taste wine.*

M. Didier had not complimented the meal, but from the way he patted his stomach and chewed his cigar, it was possible the carpet contract had already been signed in his wine-sodden mind. Coincidentally, he broached the subject in his very next comment to Mr Masood. 'Tomorrow, let us taste the soul of your nation's commerce, as tonight we have tasted its cuisine.'

'Coffee?' asked a prim-jacketed server with practised intonation.

'Yes, black.' While it was being poured, he continued, 'Helps the children's morale to see us in the factory, eh?' The coffee gradually took him back to his former, poker-faced self. He straightened his tie, but did not realize the dishevelled condition of his hair. After finishing his cup, he gestured to the server to refill it.

'I'd be only too happy to take you,' Mr Masood replied. He rose from the table to open the liquor cabinet and returned with a crystal decanter. A server placed heated snifters before each man. 'Cognac?' Mr Masood offered his guests in turn.

'Delighted,' M. Chauclet answered. M. Didier nodded.

The heat of the glasses released a dazzling bouquet. The

three men swirled and breathed their digestifs, and Mrs Masood drowned her desires in her coffee cup. Let him agree, she prayed, let the vulture agree.

And then, for the first time that evening, a smile swept across the raptor's face. His sweat had dried, his hair had somehow fallen into place, and he sat upright in high spirits and sniffed the snifter, 'I do believe our partnership will be most successful. They're a novelty in the West, handmade goods, very desirable commodities.' He glanced at his friend, the cabinet director, as though daring him, at this critical juncture, to suddenly mention the law that prohibited the import of child-made products.

But the official had a better idea, 'A toast!' He downed his drink in preparation. 'I propose it be made with Grand Marnier, in memory of its priceless success in the sauce, and in anticipation of the success of your partnership!'

Mrs Masood focused intently on the tablecloth as her husband ordered a servant to bring out the Grand Marnier. When he returned with the bottle, only a few spills were left. She cleared her throat, 'I caught one of the twins drinking it, and fired them both instantly. Sorry.' She turned graciously to the vulture, 'Will nothing else suffice?'

'Not to worry. I was enjoying my cognac anyway.'

'Yes, yes,' agreed M. Chauclet. 'More cognac will do.'

Gleefully, the men clinked their glasses. 'To the partnership!'

Mrs Masood was overwhelmed with how adeptly she had dodged a bullet, and fell into dreaming about tomorrow ... ah, tomorrow.

André nimbly guided Laila's fingers down his trousers.

Chapter Six

'Eat,' said Chaudry, breaking a piece of chapaati and reaching into his aluminum bowl for a potato. He put the morsel in Malika's mouth. She had no appetite, but she ate for him. 'Isn't it delicious?' He smiled like a parent coaxing a stubborn child.

'There's more for you,' she pointed her chin at the burner on the far side of the room, where a black pot simmered. Beside it was a charpoi with a quilt oozing bundles of soft cotton. She had been meaning to repair it, but somehow never found the time. Now Momin and the baby girl Faika huddled awkwardly in the torn mass. It was early November, normally still warm, but this year an ominous chill hung in the air. She would see to the quilt first thing in the morning.

The drape separating the room from the store flapped gently, intermittently revealing the supply of deodar delivered that day. For nearly two weeks, she had pushed thoughts of the bed Chaudry had foolishly promised to make into the furthest possible recesses of her mind, ignoring the scraps of paper on which he sketched his design. She had been preoccupied by her memory of that fateful afternoon, when she resolved to secure work at the Masood Paradise. She had not returned. In her sleep the twin Khalil's angelic face beckoned to her from inside a manhole, where she dreamed he now lived. He was begging her to clean it, for the neighbours dumped their garbage inside, oblivious that it was falling on him. She tasted the slime he daily swallowed and more than once had woken up gagging.

Yet with the physical presence of the lumber, she could no longer postpone her decision. Tomorrow her husband would begin transforming the wood according to his ludicrously complex drawings, for which both he and Momin would pay, one with his age, the other his youth. She had no choice but to return to the industrialist's home.

Chaudry continued feeding her, smiling at the way he conquered her obdurateness. She let him have this pleasure, though her mind raced, questioning how a man of nearly sixty could create a double bed in less than two months with only his hands. For he found electrical tools unsatisfying: not only did they waste precious electricity but also prevented an artist from getting close enough to his work. It was the difference between an electrical razor and a hand razor, he once tried to explain. A man could neither feel nor control the effect of the former. Having never shaved, Malika rejected the disparity.

True, she reflected, there were two pairs of hands to work with, for there was the apprentice. Talpur was a loyal, self-effacing man. But Chaudry had employed him for his personality rather than potential, and insisted on personally doing the bulk of even the hard labour. Talpur was a guest.

She frowned. He tried to wheedle away the wrinkles with

potato curry. Neither of them had spoken since her first bite, but she wondered if he guessed the reason for her sullenness. Or did he think her nothing but a pouting child?

'You should have at least taken a deposit,' she said at last, putting him to the test.

'Deposit?' He formed another morsel. Deciding it was too big, he scooped out half a potato and an onion ring.

'For the bed.' If only, this one time, she could mould him as he did that bite.

'And what good would a deposit do? She could easily demand it back. Her husband is a powerful man.' He thrust the morsel carelessly in her mouth. His good humour was disturbed and he handled the food impatiently, no longer caring how he constructed the next mouthful.

Malika was sensitive to the change. Rare were the times when she distressed him, and frequent his adoration. He complimented her dinners daily, never complaining of not having enough meat. He basked in the fragrance of her hair ('What do you use?' he pleaded, but it remained a secret), and observed with fondness how her body evolved since he first caressed it, when she was sixteen. He enjoyed all the extra touches she put around the house, like the drape she hung between the store and the room, or the flowers she brought home on the rare occasions when Mr Saeed's temperamental garden bloomed. Had she remembered to sew the quilt, he would instantly have thanked her.

But now she had trespassed into the sacred territory of his work. It was no use retreating. 'No one works without guarantee these days. If you feared the important lady couldn't be trusted, you should have refused her service. She's cheated you twice already.'

He grew angry. 'So is that why you've been grumpy all week? Don't think I haven't noticed the way you mutter into corners every time I look at you! Now I know what you've been jabbering: "My husband is too weak to conduct his own business, I should take over!" Well, you're a fool for thinking that! Who in the world would listen to *you*?'

Recognizing in his voice the venom he used for his sons, but absolutely never for her, she burst into sobs: 'You're too soft a businessman!'

He placed the aluminum bowl on the mat on which he sat, and with determined indifference, waited for her tears to subside. But when they wouldn't, he sighed. Stroking her long, aromatic hair, he whispered, 'Don't worry, my little bird.'

His tenderness was impossible to resist. She sank into the warmth of his bony embrace, and yielded to the tingle of his sensitive fingers as they brushed away her hair from wet eyes.

'Don't worry, my little bird,' he soothingly repeated, as he had only a week after their marriage, when she writhed in bed with menstrual cramps that shot through her body like electric currents hooked to her guts. 'Don't worry, my little bird,' he had said then, rubbing her limbs with foul-smelling mustard oil. Together with the sweet, hot tea he helped her sip, the massage had cured her within five minutes. She grew fond of acrid mustard, and had in fact included a dab of it in the secret shampoo he so loved.

She touched the pale, drawn skin of his cheeks, flesh twenty years older than her own but oh so childish! Nuzzling against it, she gently said, 'How can I not worry when you're cheated?'

He held her firmly, and in the closeness of those few minutes Malika was overcome with the security of their love. Yet she held her breath, knowing they could not be clasped forever.

He said, 'It's difficult for a woman to understand, since it's not she who carries the burden of her lineage. But a man is born with a promise to fulfill. Mine is that I keep alive the trade of my ancestors. It took twenty years of intense dedication to learn my father's craft, just one motif took years to ingrain. Today I'm one of the few living testaments of that tradition. I will not compromise my knowledge. I will not become one of those cheap labourers who mass-produce furniture for display at fancy showrooms! That's not what I promised. It's those men, promoted like beggars by smart-suited middlemen, who are cheated. They never have a chance to create what they are able to, but like donkeys, merely bray the same two patterns again and again. They have jobs. I have duties. We should be grateful for a customer like Mrs Masood for she never tells me how to do my work.' Breathless, he pushed her aside and rose to get water.

Alone, she shut her eyes to hide the welling tears, while her mind reeled with arguments. What about his duties to her? To his son? He sacrificed not only himself, but their entire family for *his* tradition, while the so-called 'donkeys' earned decent wages. But Chaudry, in an effort to keep the past alive, would always be anonymous. Mr Saeed, for example, had never come to him. He always went to the better-known, more expensive shops, to add to his priceless collection. Why couldn't Chaudry see Mrs Masood cared nothing for the authenticity of his craft? She merely found him easy to manoeuvre.

But Malika dared not voice her opinion. It was not fear that restrained her, but the knowledge that Chaudry had made up his mind. Trying to convert him to her point of view would be as disastrous as trying to straighten a hunchback. She dried her eyes.

He sat beside her again. 'I know it's hard for you to

understand, little bird. But my efforts are not in vain. When Momin is old enough I'll teach him these ancient skills, and if you're not a proud wife, you'll be a proud mother! He's a hard-working boy. He'll succeed, perhaps even more than I.'

Malika gazed deeply into his aged eyes, eyes like their lost son Moeez's, like the simple twin Khalil's. They were melancholy eyes, drawn to romance and tragedy, easily identified by artful opportunists like Shauqat, Jamil or Mrs Masood. At that moment Malika wanted nothing more in the world than to shield those eyes. She embraced Chaudry's narrow neck, tickled the knoll that was his Adam's apple, and combed his white beard with her fingers. 'Of course I'm proud of you,' she whispered, not knowing herself exactly what about him made her so, or if it did at all.

But he was convinced, and beamed happily. 'Show me a trick, little bird.'

With a mischievous smile, Malika stuck her pointed tongue into each nostril.

Chaudry laughed delightedly, 'Jiggle it!'

The tongue danced in her nose.

'I should call you my little lizard,' he giggled, kissing her lightly on the mouth. He held her close again. 'Did I ever tell you about my grandfather who was hired by a nawab to make a takhtposh? You know the carpenter before him was torn by tigers for not carving it to his liking. Imagine my grandfather's fear when he was hired next!' Chaudry slapped his thigh, laughing like a child. 'But he ended up making the most perfect one in the palace!'

Malika had heard this, and several other stories of Chaudry's ancestors, before. She humoured him while he told another tale about an uncle whose majestic cupboards were exalted in poems as the meeting place of a beautiful maiden and her many lovers. But then she grew tired and gently, so as not to insult him, suggested, 'If you're going to start work on that bed tomorrow, don't you think you should sleep first?'

'Ah yes, you're absolutely right,' he took a strapless wristwatch out of his kurta pocket and studied its plain white face. 'It's ten thirty. We should go to sleep, little bird.' The power of suggestion was so strong that he yawned while putting his plate over Malika's, as was his habit after every meal. 'Wash them in the morning, don't worry about anything else tonight.' He staggered into bed and shut his eyes. While falling asleep, he mumbled, 'You think too much.'

'It'll be easier to clean them now,' Malika answered, ignoring his last comment.

Chaudry had already begun to snore.

On her way to the tap outside, she glanced at Momin susurrating in his sleep, as if another voice spoke through his sparrow-like frame. She knelt beside him, trying to decipher what was uttered. She heard a range of sounds beginning with soft, windy murmuring, then dry leaves rustling, and finally a fit of furious coughing, but understood nothing.

She roused him with a drink of water, then rocked him back to sleep, praying it would be a soundless one. But beneath his wavering eyelids, the eyes rolled, and the dull murmurs began again. This time a fourth note sounded: a low, elongated mourning. She tucked his elfin chin into the dishevelled quilt, and stroked his bruised fingers. What horrid creatures rattled his sleep? Were they distorted versions of the figures he weaved, or of the children he sat beside at the loom? Were the terrible sounds he uttered the voices of those children? What did scores of five-, six-, seven- and eight-year-olds say to one another as they interlaced their youth on warp and weft?

Momin had never told her. He never returned from the factory with stories of his work or of his coworkers. He was an introvert—fearful and uncomplaining even when gasping for breath. These were the qualities Chaudry admired in him.

Chaudry had chosen Momin's name for its better-known meaning: faithful. But the day he sent the child to the factory he had said, 'It must be as God ordained, little bird. Did you know Momin also means weaver?'

As the boy slept, she caressed his feathery lashes, so fine one fell onto her fingers. It reminded her of a book that belonged to Faisal, which contained wonderful pictures of a boy no larger than a thumb. He had an impish face, with tapering eyes and ears, just like Momin. There were pictures of him confronting creatures a hundred times his size, like a giant with ugly warts on his face, an angry bull in a pasture, even a king and his richly adorned subjects. She tied the eyelash in a tiny knot of her dupatta.

Next to Momin lay Faika. Malika had stopped breast-feeding her a month ago, yet despite her early weaning, the child was strong. She slept soundly, awoke loudly and played independently. She seemed to have inherited her mother's flexibility and was recently discovering that she could stand on her head, even though she still stumbled on her feet. But Malika resented her. Momin's wages were being stored for her dowry. It was for *her* he slaved! She pulled away the baby's share of the quilt and wrapped it around Momin. The girl shivered, sneezed once, then breathed regularly again.

Malika carried the dishes to the tap outside. A golden ring encircled the moon. She scrubbed the bowls with dirt. 'Tomorrow is Friday,' she spoke to Venus. 'That means Mr

Masood will be home as well. I wonder if I'll see him? Will they hire me? How will I find time to work in three households? How will I hide it from Chaudry?' She opened the tap. As the dirt washed away, the aluminum bowls reflected the moonlight and shone like torches in the dark night. She sighed, remembering Chaudry's comment, 'You think too much.' Sometimes she grew weary of herself too.

That night Malika dreamed she entered a room damp as a wound. In the festering darkness she carried an aluminum moon, illuminating the ceiling rippling with lizards that froze in the cold, blue light. Poised rigid, with heads propped above their bodies, they were strangely exquisite.

On the floor her bare feet popped objects soft and sticky, and she heard a hiss, as of punctured balloons. One by one they popped like blue bottles. Slime oozed under her feet, and she waved her arms to keep from slipping, shaking the seamless moon, jolting the petrified lizards. On her feet, the slime congealed like fish guts and the smell of Empress Market settled on the still air. She heard the delighted shrieks of Faisal, and then he was beside her, sucking on a milk bottle, yearning for a fishy playmate. But as he bent to pick one, he vanished.

In her sleep, Malika rubbed her blistered feet together and moaned for slippers.

She delved further into the sore. At its centre, along with the frequent hissing of pierced jellyfish, sounded a dull throb, and to its rhythm the room itself beat. Here her moon gradually faded. Dawn approached. Black turned translucent red, revealing an intricate structure of pipes and ropes that connected the floor and ceiling of the pulsing chamber. Stealthily, she crept over and between the construction, recognizing at once that disrupting its harmony would upset her dream.

In her sleep, her eyes flickered with the strain of preserving it.

And then she saw, hunkered beneath lizards that crept again as the moon disappeared, thumb-sized creatures building the tubes. They cowered at the sight of her, shielding their pitted faces with distended fingers. But the lizards loomed ominously, thumping their tails to the dull throbbing of the room, and the creatures, sucking tumid snot-coated lips, returned to work.

Without daring to look, she understood the popping jellyfish beneath her soles were these ugly bodies. In her sleep, she mourned for the ones she had killed, and gouged furiously at the blisters on her feet. When they bled, she whimpered, for it was the blood of the murdered children, whose kin quivered feverishly in her presence, beneath God-like lizards, and what pumped in steady rhythm were not pipes nor tubes but the veins and arteries of a retted heart.

When she awoke, the moon had vanished and dawn had broken.

It was Friday, Momin's day off from the factory. He usually spent it in Chaudry's shadow, rising with him for Fajr, reciting passages from the Quran, then helping him with his newest project. At midday, they bathed for prayers at the mosque, and returned for the weekly mutton palau lunch that Malika, who also had the day free, spent the morning preparing.

But this Friday she lay in bed. Her husband and son prayed under the salmon sky. Faika howled for breakfast. Her dream hung over the day, making her listless and moody. She had no incentive to converse with God, nor to feed the baby. Instead, she peered at her son's shrunken body kneeling toward the kabbah, and wondered when he had stopped growing. He was nearly six, but barely three feet tall. Was it the angle or did his head, hands and feet really comprise the entire length of his body? Did squatting at the loom stunt his growth or was he a congenital dwarf? She shuddered, for the way he squinted at the rising sun reminded her of the cowering creatures in her dream, and she wished he would get up, brush his knees free of the lowly stance, and standing tall, defy his duties for the day. Yet she herself remained in bed, exhausted, her mind tossing over confused images of a sleep that left the taste of blisters on her tongue.

Between sobs and hiccups, Faika watched her mother tear the bloodied corners of a sheet and wrap her mangled feet. She sucked the tears off her pink lips and whimpered, for her belly ached. Then she examined her own feet, the plump heels and round toes that her fingers could tickle, and that her mouth too could reach. Her moist gums wrapped around both big toes and she suckled. Her legs framed her head like wings and she chittered like a bat.

So that Chaudry would not notice, Malika covered her bandaged feet with socks that Saima had given her. Finally, she rose. While making tea and parathas for breakfast, she heard her son and husband recite: 'I swear by the Day of Resurrection; and I swear by the self-reproaching conscience.'

Faika smelt the cloves, fresh bread, butter and sugar. She released her soggy toes, sapped of all flavour, and cried again.

'We can help ourselves,' said Chaudry, entering the stove-warmed room. 'Why don't you feed her?'

Ignoring him, Malika sat Momin down and tore bite-size morsels of the hottest paratha onto his plate. He swallowed indifferently, without chewing, looking away at the pariah kites soaring nonchalantly in the pale sky that only half an hour ago had been tinged with the colour of Malika's dream. He wheezed softly.

'The cold air is bad for him,' Malika said to Chaudry. 'Now that winter is approaching, you should pray indoors.'

'It's never too cold for His glory,' Chaudry snapped. He took his plate to Faika, who howled and squirmed as he put her on his lap. Once secure in his embrace, her eyes opened and she whimpered complaints about her mother through pouting lips. 'I know, I know,' Chaudry soothed, puckering his mouth next to hers.

Let them babble together, Malika thought. For Momin's sake, she smiled pleasantly and tried to engage him in conversation. 'In winter, we'll see ducks flying east to the lake. Maybe some day we can go to watch them.' Then she regretted having said so, for when would they ever find the time?

Momin followed the flight of the birds with deathly calm. She knew he wanted to be alone, but insisted, 'Look at the crow.' She pointed to one hopping on a drainage pipe, trying to drink from it while simultaneously chasing away the others, who flapped their wings and grew rowdy in defence. 'They must be his uncles, the way they scold him!'

In silence, he watched the scavengers ascend to the sun with elastic ease. There they floated, without even a flutter. His spirits seemed to lift with them, making life bearable.

Desperately, she asked, 'Want to see a trick?' Without waiting for an answer, she opened her mouth and her tongue vanished down her throat.

Reluctantly, he pried himself free of the window. His eyes momentarily grew when he saw her, but not with the wondrous revelation of last winter, when he had first felt his mobile lower jaw, and his mother had turned into a flamingo. He was older now, and his eyes dilated in disbelief, as though, after being in the sun all day, they suddenly faced darkness. His plumy lashes flickered as they had last night, when she brushed them softly with her loving fingertips. Was it her he dreamed of when he moaned? Perhaps the nightmares that haunted him nightly were not of the children in the factory, nor of the pictures in their carpets, nor even of their flatulent boss. They were simply of her.

Now that she had her son's attention, she felt like a member of the flock of uncle-crows, yapping foolishly at the youth who merely wanted to drink independently of them. Winded with grief, she withdrew to prepare lunch.

Chaudry was tearing open Faika's paratha and mashing the potato filling so she could suck it down. He stuffed her wet, toothless mouth with as much joy as he had Malika's last night, before their quarrel. Faika drooled with satisfaction. Chaudry repeatedly scooped the mush off her chin, back into the pink cove of her mouth. 'Soon you'll have teeth,' he cooed. 'How fast you grow!'

The sky turned a nondescript grey as Malika forced herself on with the day.

Chapter Seven

Mrs Masood rejoiced at the sound of water flowing freely from the garden hose. To be closer to the melody, she opened the windows of her living room. The gardeners were digging trenches and pits, and did not need the water. But she enjoyed the waste. It made the memory of herself as a little girl—watching the desert sand frolic like fireflies, turn into itself, and abruptly change its course so that it blew furiously into her eyes—seem very, very far away.

It was ten thirty. Her husband was guiding M. Didier on a tour around the factory. Laila was at the hairdresser's. Tufail was in his quarters. The sweeperess and dhobi had left. Very slowly, she opened the chir cabinet, freeing the perfume of sweet grass from its felt lining. The doors creaked delightfully, indicating she would find something terrifying and mysterious inside. She peeped through the cabinet door, imagining it to be the entrance to a dark cavern, inside which glistened the jewels:

bottles tall and lean, round and squat, with contents rolling lazily up their sides as her fingers trembled. She chose Harvey's Bristol Cream and carried it, along with a port glass shaped like a tulip, stealthily to the sandalwood table. The cabinet door shut softly behind her.

She sat on the edge of the divan with a dupatta pinned carefully to her head and smelt the sherry. Its thick scent mingled with the perfume of the sandalwood and the sweet song of free-flowing water. In her mind's eye there formed an image of her husband and his friends at the dining table, all with thirsty, hangdog eyes and lolling tongues as she nonchalantly poured herself wine that she alone had the power to deny them. The picture so tickled Mrs Masood that she threw off her slippers and delved with her bare toes into the warmth of the burgundy rug.

Once she had overheard her husband explain the rug's floral design, how it was reminiscent of seventeenth-century Mughal patterns, which were in turn modelled after the gardens of Persia. The rectangular walled gardens, irrigated by pools and shaded by trees, were meant to represent paradise. It had been after she discovered this bit of carpet history that Mrs Masood had named her house the Masood Paradise.

Mr Masood had also said that Mughal patterns were often naturalistic, with animals and hunting scenes. And this had tickled her fancy, since it was on a hunting expedition that Mr Masood had stumbled upon her. It was also no coincidence that the rug's background was predominantly wine red. Her life had such order. Everything was in its place, just like all the objects in her living room, and the topiary outside. She tilted her glass so the amber liquid brushed her tongue like velvet, like the silken wool closing around her foot.

For the first time in her life, she became acutely aware of the space inside her mouth. When in his characteristically rough, inattentive style, Mr Masood would probe inside it with his tongue, she was too small for him. But now the space grew infinitesimally, every millimetre charged with sensual delight. Her tongue, previously a rusty bridge for food to hurry across, became a breathing ocean too vast to escape. The wine crystallized in the pockets of her taste buds like pearls in a shell. The pearls sank soundlessly to the spongy depths of her tongue, to the seabed, and only then was she satisfied of having sucked every flavour and every pleasure from every molecule swimming inside her. She took another sip, and another, till there was no telling how many teardrop glasses were consumed.

She rolled onto her belly on the plush divan, hoisted up her kurta and loosened the drawstring of her shalwar. Her dupatta rolled down her naked back lightly, like gossamer. She focused all her attention on locating it in places never touched before: the soft crevice under her knees, her instep, armpits, the nape of her neck, the deep crescent of her buttocks. Then she piled it between her legs and ground it gently.

Outside the French windows, water rushed merrily from the garden hose where Malika stood gaping at the picture inside the living room. She had been banging on the kitchen door for several minutes, but when no one answered, had walked to the front. There the gardeners had told her that the mistress was sure to be inside, and pointed at the windows. So she walked onto the patio, and found, to her utter amazement, the haughty, neatly groomed, omnipotent Mrs Masood squeezing a full, white breast while heaving over the bulge of her dupatta, grunting like an animal.

Malika held her breath for the windows were open and she was terrified of being discovered. The pins holding Mrs

Masood's hair—'the finest I've ever seen,' Chaudry had stammered, intimidated by *this*—tumbled silently onto the carpet. She stared at them fixedly while trying to think, rubbing her cheeks to wipe away the colour flooding them. Never before had she been so ashamed, not even the first night Chaudry had undressed her, and she had seen her naked body as if through his eyes, wondering if it were dirty or clean. When he had been satisfied and rolled off her, silent but for the panting, she had secretly promised never to see herself through him again.

But now she was doing worse. She was witnessing another woman, a woman of importance, engage in an act more intimate than sex between husband and wife, and more illicit than between lovers. She swallowed hard, tugging at her elbows, as if the feel of her own skin, dignified under clothing, could give solace.

The gardeners leaned on their spades, watching her. Unable to bear the consequence of other men discovering Mrs Masood's naked, lascivious body, the body that was so like her own, she approached them before they could her.

'Did you find the begum?' the one who had told her to check in the living room asked.

'Uh,' Malika coloured again. 'No. Perhaps I should wait a while.'

He shrugged. 'She never goes out, except for shopping. But I saw Laila bibi leave alone so she must be in.'

Malika could not answer. She twisted her feet sideways, and placed one on top of the other in an effort to diminish in size.

Another worker with paan-stained lips laughed, 'You're flat-footed as a chicken!'

The others circled around her and chimed in, 'Bet she clucks like one too!'

'Get back to work,' the first gardener ordered. He turned to her, 'They mean no harm.'

Unhurriedly, still nudging each other to look in her direction, the others began shovelling again. Malika stayed near the kind man. He jumped into a trench and tossed dirt onto the surface, careful to avoid her. The fresh scent of the earth was calming. She smiled down at him, 'What are you going to plant here?'

He wiped his sweat-filled eyes with the back of a soiled hand. The veins of his thick neck bulged like ropes and the sunlight accentuated the muscles of his perfectly sculpted, shirtless torso. 'It's a crazy idea, really,' he rolled his grey Pathan eyes, molten in the sun. 'For bibi Laila's wedding, they want the whole garden planted with boxwood bigger than my house!' He spat. Malika found herself enchanted with his frank manner, tiger eyes and sinuous bust. 'The manager tried to tell the begum these things take years to grow but she insisted on having them by December. So we're transplanting them. If you ask me, the garden was more beautiful before than it can ever be with hedges shaped like ducks and deer with weak roots.'

'Ducks and deer?' Malika asked.

'It's costing her a fortune,' the Pathan resumed shovelling. 'We're having to hire tractors to carry the load.' He stuck his spade deep into the soil and leaned on its handle thoughtfully. Malika noticed that his stomach was even tighter from this angle. He continued, 'Of course, I've nothing to complain about. This contract pays better than all the ones I've had this year put together. Still, it's a shame for the flowers.'

The sun slowly climbed to its zenith. Over the Pathan's right shoulder remained a solitary bush of crimson jetrofa. A tiny sunbird flitted like a bee from petal to petal. Malika's heart ached as she remembered Momin's indifference to her earlier this morning, as he drifted with the pariah kites over the rooftops. Yet she was grateful there was still something that could give him pleasure. If Chaudry's family had been gardeners, she thought, then Momin too would have been initiated into the profession. He could spend his life surrounded by the creatures he loved. Instead, at this very moment, he was trapped in a room full of splinters, and tomorrow he would return to one of burr.

The Pathan pointed to the western end of the garden where a stone walkway swerved to the back of the house. 'That's where the wedding banquet is to be served. Under a tent, thank God, so there'll be no room to plant giant yews like she wanted. The manager flatly refused. Then you know what she asked for?' He leaned further into the spade and looked her boldly in the face. She stumbled back. 'A canopy of privet as the tent, replete with white flowers, since white's the colour of a maghribi wedding. You do know Laila bibi's marrying a ferangi? They say he's converting but I'm not so sure. I've heard there'll be liquor at the banquet. That's why she wants it hidden in a tent, which, incidentally, she finally agreed to have made of cloth.'

Confused images of bushy ducks and deer and secret drinking in a white tent fluttered across Malika's mind, already burdened with the knowledge of Mrs Masood masturbating on a gold divan.

'The cook Tufail says he's seen Mr Masood drink with his own eyes,' the Pathan was saying. 'I'm told there's a cabinet full of it.' His eyes glittered like topaz. She thought of Moeez, once stalwart and self-assured like this handsome gardener, reduced to a whimpering puddle by drugs. 'I'm surprised your husband lets you come to a household like this. From what I've heard, with all the wealth they have, they don't even pay their servants well. And she,' he raised an eyebrow toward the French windows, 'even beats them. Smacked the last two straight out of the house. But she should know better. Youth is fiery and seeks revenge.' He nodded knowingly like a wizened sage.

Malika looked closely at him, wondering at his age. But the face was timeless, like a gem. Then she stared dejectedly at her feet, still positioned one over the other, remembering the twins flung out of the kitchen door. She suddenly grew unspeakably guilty for being here, and looked at the gate, out of which she could still leave and never return.

The Pathan seemed to sense her sorrow and smiled amiably. 'Your luck may be different.' He thrust his hip provocatively to the side, more like a playboy than a wise old man.

Malika blushed. 'Maybe the begum is back. I'll check again.' She could feel his eyes on her back as she returned to the living room.

The window was still ajar. Mrs Masood had dressed, yet remained sunk in the divan. Hairpins mottled the carpet. Eyeliner smeared her lower lids, giving her the appearance of someone who had not slept in weeks. She blinked dully at Malika without noticing her.

After weeks of swallowing the hatred she bore her, now that Malika finally had the opportunity to confront Mrs Masood, she wondered what course to take. Belligerence? The woman was, after all, alone in the house and in her present state of lethargy it would be easy to crack her neck and run with the booty! She could use it to put Momin in school, buy him books and new clothes, and even continue stocking for Faika's dowry so Chaudry would never know. Or should she be obsequious and fall on her knees? Smother the woman's fair and lovely feet with kisses? Insist she use her clout with Mr Masood, so he would release the factory children and offer their families handsome compensations, including schooling?

Mrs Masood stared longingly out of the French windows at her torn paradise, more like a prisoner than a wife with clout. Gone was the confident, bombastic demeanour of the powdered woman in Chaudry's store. The bejewelled fingers that had then tossed Chaudry a measly one thousand rupees now fidgeted with her crumpled dupatta as though they had been cheated.

At last Malika's presence seemed to register with her and she asked in a heavy voice, 'Who are you?'

Malika cracked her toes, struck by the absurdity of the question. The woman who had snatched so much from her did not even know she existed. Stranger still was that Malika felt herself to have the advantage. The course to take was neither aggression nor flattery, but the one Mrs Masood offered on her own: ambiguity.

'I'm Soomla,' she smiled secretly, thinking of the legendary Sindhi princess renowned for her magical powers. 'I was wondering if you needed a maid.'

Mrs Masood eyed her sluggishly. 'Well,' she forced herself up on an elbow and moaned. After massaging her temples for another minute, she sighed, 'You can begin by pouring me a glass of cold water. The kitchen's behind you. And find some Disprin as well.'

Malika returned quickly with both requests. Mrs Masood popped the tablets in her mouth and downed the water in one gulp. 'That's better,' she said to herself, putting the glass on the sandalwood table.

Malika turned pale. Thus far, she had been so surprised by Mrs Masood's appearance that, though vaguely aware of standing in a room full of valuables, she had not registered any of them, particularly not the one that had brought her here in the first place. Now she saw nothing but the table. She touched its floral border, her fingers remembering how Chaudry's had painstakingly breathed life into each stalk, petal and vine. She smelt her finger: it was the perfume he had brought with him to bed at the end of each day spent shaping the work. He had been exhausted yet proud, like she had been after giving birth to each of their three sons. And tonight his eyes would burn with the same light of self-assurance, after wasting his time on a wedding bed that promised no fruition.

Mrs Masood's head was clearing. The peasant before her presented a welcome diversion, for as her headache subsided a greater pain steadily took its place. It grew with the knowledge that, in one swift gesture, she had eradicated the sole purpose of her life: to obey her husband. As if to prove it, the evidence—a near-empty bottle of Harvey's and a sticky glass—gaped at her in brazen triumph. A cloying sweetness settled like a parasite on her tongue, the very tongue that minutes ago had afforded her boundless pleasure. Now she wished to be rid of it, to never speak and never taste, for only then could her sin be forgotten. Yet the more she thought of it, the closer the sweetness tugged, till she feared it was as permanent as the yellow mustard in every follicle of her grandmother's hair. She writhed at the thought of the old woman who had surely been a witness to her crime.

To suppress her fear, she stared hard at Malika, still mesmerized by the table. At social gatherings, wives of important men often advised Mrs Masood to employ female rather than male servants, remarking that women had a greater capacity for hard work and quiet endurance. Yet, but for the washerwoman and sweeperess, all the servants in her house were men. She feared her husband would seek them as he once did her.

But Malika would not present any danger: her mouth was large, nose too sharp, and her eyes did not taper. In her mind, she stripped off her clothes. Beneath the muslin dupatta casually cloaking her shoulders appeared swarthy breasts, muscular shoulders and narrow hips. She peeled away the shalwar as well: mercifully, the legs had not been treated with turmeric paste to lighten their colour, nor with wheat to soften their texture. And there was something indescribably off with her feet, swollen like the roots of a banyan tree.

She sat up abruptly, unable to believe what she saw. Malika cracked her ankles and agitatedly twisted her feet, first sideways then backwards. She pursued Mrs Masood with her eyes, drawing silently, ferociously nearer, till at last she pounced, 'Where did you get the table?'

Mrs Masood mopped the sweat off her face and mumbled a prayer, begging her grandmother for forgiveness.

Receiving no response, Malika leaned over the table and smelt the bottle of red liquid resting on it. Remembering the gardener's warning that there was liquor in the house, she wrinkled her nose with disgust.

Mrs Masood watched Malika's face grow gelid with disapproval and she delved further into the divan, pleading, 'I won't do it again.'

Malika wondered at Mrs Masood's servile tone but was too distracted to give it much thought. She repeated her question, 'Where did you get the table?'

'I'm thirsty,' Mrs Masood choked on the sickening sweetness inflating her tongue like a balloon. 'Help me! Shut the window! I've been found! The churail has me!'

Malika stared at her inverted feet and, perceiving herself through Mrs Masood's eyes, suddenly saw the churail. She burst into triumphant laughter: Chaudry had repeatedly asked that she break her habit, swearing it would cause her difficulty. Instead, it had made her path easier! She studied the feet objectively, like Chaudry examined his first sketches, and concluded that they were diamonds in the rough: coarse from walking and scarred by last night's dream, but so tough that they caused mountains to crumble, roles to invert.

'Forgive me! Forgive me!' Mrs Masood gasped breathlessly.

'Why should I?' Malika teased. Leaving Mrs Masood to find a suitable answer, she again admired the table's unique symmetry: vines twirling like smoke, caressing petals that varied in size and shape according to Chaudry's mood. Though she had watched him set the pattern, seeing it again made her realize that it was too visceral to memorize. Last night he had chided other carpenters for their predictability, and now, for a brief instant, she understood his pride: there would never be another mould like this. She thought of Momin, of the fact that there would never be another life like his, and she studied Mrs Masood: there were too many like her.

'If you do as I say,' Malika offered stiffly, 'there's a chance I'll forgive you.'

'What?' Mrs Masood asked eagerly. 'What can I do?'

Malika sat beside her on the divan. She pulled her knees up under her chin so the twisted feet all but touched Mrs Masood. 'First, hire me as your maid. I expect a modest salary, say four thousand rupees a month, to be paid in weekly installments. In return I'll dedicate eight hours of hard work every week, five of those on Fridays, during which I'll dust, clean, sweep, cook and so on, as long as I don't have to stay overtime.'

Mrs Masood nodded hopefully, though a twinge of doubt pierced her stomach: how would she wring this amount from Mr

Masood, who would laugh at the prospect of a masi for so much?

'Good,' Malika continued. 'Now, tell me truthfully, how much do you think that table is worth?'

For an instant, a jubilant smile swept across Mrs Masood's face, reminding Malika of the crafty woman of the store. 'That table? A poor fool made it on order for one thousand rupees! It's easily worth five thousand!' She forgot herself and laughed.

'Evil woman,' Malika breathed down her neck, her feet carving stormy crescents in the air beneath Mrs Masood's nose. 'Twice you've cheated the faithful carpenter, once with the cabinet, then the table. In fact, *thrice* if you include those statuettes.' Malika gazed for an instant at the sleek, dark bodies near the divan. Chaudry had given his youth to them! She spat, 'And in your wretched heart you've already fooled him a fourth time.'

Mrs Masood gaped, wondering how Malika could possibly know.

Malika was quick to respond, 'A churail knows more about you than you could wish. Be advised: tomorrow, return to the carpenter's store and pay him his due, including another five thousand rupees as deposit on the bed he slaves to build your daughter for her wedding. When complete, it'll be the most desired article in the entire subcontinent, enough to make martyred kings curse their death. If your payment is honourable, your daughter's ferangi husband will never seek another, and I'll leave you forever. But if unjust, the watchful spirits of the bedstead will prevent your daughter's marriage from ever being consummated, while I'll haunt you till death.'

'I'll go tomorrow,' Mrs Masood hastily promised, beads of perspiration mottling her brow as she anxiously prayed to God for assistance in guessing the 'honourable' amount, and in persuading her husband to provide it.

'It's time to speak of your other sins,' Malika pointed to the Harvey's. 'Go to the cabinet. Return this bottle and bring me a full one.'

Again Mrs Masood felt her tongue rise like dough in her mouth. She yearned to tear it, piece by fermenting piece, to dispel the smothering sugariness once and for all. Instead, she followed Malika's instructions, this time paying little attention to the cabinet's creaking doors, or its dark, khas-scented interior. She pulled out the first wine bottle before her.

'Open it,' Malika, who knew nothing about corkscrews, ordered.

Having witnessed her husband wield the tool umpteen times, Mrs Masood adeptly popped the cork.

'Bring a clean glass and sit beside me again.'

Mrs Masood obeyed, reminding Malika of the way she had rushed about for her barely half an hour ago, carrying water and Disprin. Her heart raced at finding her world suddenly so changed, and she grew so disorientated that for an instant it was as if she were a character in the storybooks Saima read to Faisal at bedtime. It was those make-believe people, like the bold thumb-sized boy, whose lives were charged with impossible events in every page. Such things did not happen to people reading the story.

Mrs Masood tentatively settled beside her. Malika took the gilt-edged goblet from her hands, filled it with wine and handed it back, commanding coolly, 'Drink it.'

Mrs Masood leaned back. Her head reeled with nausea from the fumes. 'Please, anything but this. You see, a terrible sensation has overcome me. My tongue swells, my throat itches and my head swims like a spinning wheel. When I was a child, my grandmother would tell me stories of djinns living in a human body, gnawing at it with iron jaws from the inside out, leaving their victims forever burning with thirst. That is how I am now. This is punishment enough. More wine will only feed my . . . '

'I have heard,' Malika brusquely interrupted, 'that men will utter magic spells before they drink. They even have a name for it—in English. You must know?'

Mrs Masood stuttered. 'You mean,' she said in English, 'a toast?'

'A toast.' Malika tasted the foreign word on her tongue. She thrust the goblet closer to Mrs Masood and smiled. 'That must be it. I insist on a toast.'

The wine's odour crackled up Mrs Masood's nose like a burning ember, flaring again in the darkness of her blood. The only toasts she knew were those made by her husband and his friends, toasts in English that Soomla would not understand. And what did it matter now anyway? 'To prosperity,' she muttered. 'To partnership. To the native leftovers in the refrigerator.' As she forced down the spirit, sweat pasted her skin and the cool gold rim of her goblet ignited with the heat from her lips.

Malika watched. Her glee waned. Instead of a defeated Mrs Masood, she saw Moeez. He had broken steadily like a poltroon, his every desire manoeuvred by Shauqat, himself a puppet to some wealthy drug lord. She wondered how the tycoon invested his wealth. In land? Politics? Carpets?

Absently refilling the goblet she passed it again under Mrs Masood's nose, picturing Moeez beneath a moonless sky, balancing on a rickety boat off the Makran coast. His clothes were damp and his arms laced with spume as he reached helplessly for the dock, where Shauqat rolled in shadow with cotton bags full of white dust.

Part Two:
Tom Thumb's Minnow

Chapter Eight

The carpenter Chaudry was sanding the fourth leg of the wedding bed when Mrs Masood walked into his store. All the other furniture was piled against the wall as if business had been suspended for this project. The floor was strewn with sandpaper, clamps, planes, ripsaws, coping saws, cans of varnish, brushes and design plans. She trod very carefully past the rubble without meeting his eyes.

Malika peeped through the curtain. The bare-bottomed Faika raced on all fours to attract her mother's attention. She took a tin pot and wore it like a hat. She tapped on it with a spoon. 'Shh!' Malika scolded, her eyes burning with anticipation.

Mrs Masood's face was shamefully lowered. Her once-commanding fingers now curled inward like hangnails. It was impossible to believe, thought Malika, just how well her plan was working. She shut her eyes. Her mind blazed with triumph, ambition, but most of all with fear. It was the kind of fear that only haunts those with an advantage: the fear of losing it. Now that Malika had the upper hand, there could be nothing more painful than falling to the bottom again.

It was this pain that she recognized in Mrs Masood. The once sprucely attired, heavily made-up wife of the wealthy industrialist now cowered like the children in her husband's factory. Malika recalled how she had seen her, barely three weeks ago, in the doorway to the street. She felt again the rage that had bewitched her then. But she had forced Mrs Masood back to the scene of her crime to pay. Now it was Mrs Masood who was bewitched.

Faika again waddled toward her mother, then changed her mind. She sat at a safe distance on the tin pot and began humming the barely decipherable tune that crackled on Chaudry's radio.

O Saqi! Give me two full cups. One from yourself,
the other a gift from God . . .

Mrs Masood pressed her temples. The music was like a network of the finest cracks splitting inside her. Dizzily, she longed to be back in her living room, reclining on her gold divan with two full cups. The song taunted her. It was a cruel, cruel world.

'Good morning,' Chaudry bowed. 'I'm afraid the bed is not at all ready. You did, if you'll forgive my reminding you, allow till the eve of our Quaid's birthday. It's only mid-November.'

An idiot, thought Mrs Masood. The carpenter was a jabbering fool. If he only conducted his business with an iota of sense, she would not be in this mess. He smiled at her, slurping with good cheer. 'That's not why I've come,' she answered haughtily, attempting to mimic her lost superiority. But her head throbbed, and her confidence dwindled. She had tied a dupatta tightly around her temples, hoping the pressure would alleviate her headache. But the rayon cloth rubbed her hair spray and produced a series of electric currents that made her skin crawl.

Fill my cup to the brim; fill a river in each drop.

The singer's chapped voice nipped her flesh like a sandstorm in the desert. She staggered.

Chaudry rushed to her aid. 'What's the matter, begum? Please sit down.' He dragged a rickety chair under her. 'Please,' he repeated, his brows furrowed with concern.

Malika rolled her eyes irritably. She could not have known that at that moment, both she and Mrs Masood felt exactly the same way about Chaudry.

Though wanting nothing more than to leave, Mrs Masood sat down. It was strange, she thought, how her mind was in opposition to her actions. Only yesterday she had reflected on how well all the events of her life were arranged, like an even design, like a carpet. Then she had sinned, and been caught. Now she had no control over her life: the design was free flowing, ever changing. She was the pawn, not the queen. It was like being in the desert again.

'Perhaps,' Chaudry smiled, 'I can show you the progress on Laila bibi's bed. Is that why you've come?' She did not answer. He resumed happily, 'It's understandable, of course, if you're curious. And I like nothing more than describing the process.' He clapped his hands and moved toward the bed, fingering and tapping it as he spoke. 'Well, as you can see, the cut of the frame is one hundred per cent clean. God has blessed me with eyes sharper than a trisquare, though,' he giggled, 'I don't even know what that is!' His fingers flitted like wings. 'And remark the quality of the grain. There is no finer deodar in any store. Smell it! Smell it!' He rubbed the wood's surface like an herb and held his finger under her nose.

Sometimes I've drunk from my pain, sometimes from
my thirst;
Always with nothing to gain, but an open heart and an
empty purse!

Bristling with nausea, Mrs Masood pushed Chaudry's finger aside. She looked about her with thirsty, red-rimmed eyes and began scratching like a dog with fleas.

Faika ceased humming. Imitating the customer, she began scratching her chubby legs and arms, then tickled her belly, laughing with pleasure. 'Funny!' she squealed, till Malika gave her a tight smack. She howled, and Chaudry looked toward the drape. Malika grabbed Faika and quickly ducked away. 'Be quiet,' she pleaded. The child touched the warm, sturdy arms that held her, and took to scratching them instead. Malika peeped again.

'I invested,' continued Chaudry, 'in a brand new backsaw.' He lifted a thin rectangular blade by its metal hand bar. 'For the joints. Aren't they perfect? Level and precise. Next I'll be staining the frame and then begin the part I've been waiting for.' He paused. 'It's not that I don't pay equal attention to all the steps, it's just that, well, it's like having children you know,' he lowered his voice. 'There's always one that excites you most.' He smiled, and spoke in a normal voice again, 'That would be the headboard. Wait till you see the pattern for it!'

Malika angrily released Faika. 'Your brother's going to school,' she said to the bewildered girl. 'Whether your father wants it or not, your brother's going to school. Why should he slave for you? Tell your father to earn a decent living and you'll have your dowry!' She folded her arms and looked away, gazing

78

determinedly at the bowed woman in the rickety chair. Underneath Faika, in the tin pot, drummed drops of water. The child looked up sheepishly, but happily, for there was nothing like relieving a full bladder.

Mrs Masood believed she was back in the Cholistan Desert, carrying water from a toba that was quickly drying. She and her family would have to move again. The rains were late. But oh, she was so tired of walking! On and on, across the flat, scorched dhaar, then over the sandy tibas where cobras slept. And here were the tracks of a sidewinder, crescent after crescent, as the beast rolled on its flank. A snake without a slither was like a man without a limb. The tracks would soon be lost to the fiery desert wind, the loo. She wanted to sit, to never roam again. To lounge on a gold divan from where sprinklers could be seen wheeling steadily: click, click, click. And rain everywhere. But instead she was falling, just like her grandmother said she would, into a pit of nothingness, a sinner with a rotting, tumescent tongue.

Then, in a moment of recollection, Mrs Masood precariously opened her purse and produced a wad of rupees. Her husband had refused to give her money, saying no masi was worth so much. She had been forced to take it from her daughter's dowry. She was adding to her sin. But what was the choice? The witch Soomla would be watching.

'I believe this is yours,' Mrs Masood placed the money in Chaudry's hands.

That's the way! Malika smiled, enjoying Chaudry's confusion.

'No, begum sahib, you owe me nothing,' he pleaded.

Fool! Malika's feet twitched.

'Apparently I do,' Mrs Masood sighed and rose.

Chaudry pushed the money back into her pallid hands.

Give it today!
Who knows what the jaam tells
If by tomorrow my life is snuffed?

'Take it!' the customer snapped. 'Four thousand more for the sandalwood table, plus deposit on the bed. You were a fool to settle for less.' Swallowing what remained of her pride, she stormed outside.

'Well!' Chaudry confusedly counted the money. 'Well!' he repeated, his mouth wide open. He scratched his long, white beard. 'She looked unwell.' He sat on the rickety chair, still warm from Mrs Masood's body, and recounted the cash. Then his face slowly melted into the boyish, uncertain, almost guilty smile that always melted Malika. She longed to rush out and tickle his wiry beard, to suggest they celebrate by going somewhere, just the two of them, as they used to before he had exiled their sons. Instead she waited for him to call her.

Then Chaudry smacked his thigh and laughed loudly, 'Little bird! Look what God has given!'

Malika paused long enough to make it seem like she was coming from further behind the curtain. Her face was aptly bewildered. 'What, janoo?' Faika stumbled out too, but tripped. Deciding she would make better headway upside down, she flipped onto her hands, humming again.

Forbid not what gives me life, forbid those who would
take it.
Some men drink blood, I ask only for wine . . .

Chaudry spun them both in his arms, 'Nine thousand rupees! For Faika's dowry!' He wheeled them faster, unable to see his wife's face fall and feet swing backwards. Unable to hear her scream in silent outrage: this is not why I practically risked my life.

'Funny!' squealed Faika again, as Chaudry turned with the speed of his own happiness.

Malika sobbed, afraid of being at the bottom again.

Chapter Nine

With Mrs Masood's first instalment, Malika took Momin to a doctor. The cloaked physician, herself looking rather anaemic, prescribed a slew of antibiotics, ointments, syrups, inhalers and vitamins for Momin. When Malika asked what was wrong with him, she stumbled over a long list of ailments with names that seemed unfamiliar even to her. Frustrated, Malika asked why his fingers were crooked and his spine arched like a scimitar.

The doctor was faintly amused by the metaphor. 'His bones are permanently damaged. He has been seriously wounded at his job. Hence the, uh, as you so vividly put it, scimitar shape.'

'Well,' Malika frowned, hoping the next time she would be told something *scientific*. 'What about his sleep? He moans and picks imaginary lint from the air. What does that have to do with his bones?'

The doctor scribbled another prescription. 'He has suffered mental as well as physical trauma. As a mother, you should have known better than to subject him to that.'

Malika rose in a huff.

While beckoning the next patient inside, the doctor added, 'I've included pills that will help him sleep. You might want to take some yourself.'

Though indignant about the doctor's comments, a few days later Malika was pleased to note that the medicines actually helped. During the day, Momin's coughing fits grew less frequent and while he slept, the restlessness diminished.

She then inquired about nearby schools and discovered classes would begin in January. I should be able to enroll him then, she mused happily.

To ensure that Chaudry did not grow suspicious, she continued applying henna on Momin's old cuts. And he still left home every morning for the five-thirty bus to the factory, but only Malika knew he never took it. What she did not know, however, was where he went, for her job at Mr Saeed's and the hours spent with Mrs Masood still kept them apart. While grateful for the free time Momin could finally enjoy, she regretted it was unsupervised, and worried: what if Chaudry's belief that freedom bred deceit in children proved true? So one brisk November morning, though feeling guilty for abandoning his children, she resolved to resign from Mr Saeed's.

As she approached his study to submit her notice, she thought of their last meeting months ago in the spring. A smartly attired dealer had marched into the house bearing a stuffed armadillo. Its armour was studded with rubies.

'It belonged to a Maharani,' the dealer had announced. Malika had marvelled at the way the man's stiff, glossy shoes reflected the armadillo's front claws, and wished he would flip the body over so the rubies could dazzle in them as well.

'Mr Saeed has sent for it, all the way from Patna. Please inform him of its arrival.'

She had hurried to his study door and repeated the message through the keyhole. Surprisingly, Mr Saeed emerged almost at once, his arms extended to embrace the ancient mammal.

'Unbelievable!' For the first time in all the years that she had known him, his ashen face came to life. 'Who would have thought?' He fingered the scintillating gems, poking his face inside the armadillo's snout.

'It's there,' the dealer nodded, and curiosity had gotten the better of Malika, who practically pushed Mr Saeed aside to see what was *there*: a blinding star set in a worm-shaped tongue.

Mr Saeed was pleased with her astonishment. 'Indeed, it's the sharpest diamond that even I've seen.' He patted the snout meditatively. 'It's said the Maharani fed the creature from a gold purse shaped like a termite nest. He would probe inside it with his diamond-studded tongue. The diamond would crawl with ants and worms. Fascinating, what?'

Malika drew away. The queen's love for the punctured thing was wicked, and Mr Saeed's enthusiasm shocking.

But he continued, 'No one knows where the Maharani found him, since the mammal is no longer known in the Old World. It was rumoured that she had it smuggled across the ocean. Or that the mammal had once existed in the Cholistan Desert, and that this was an indigenous specimen, the last of its line.

'She kept the one-hundred-and-forty-pounder on a leash like a dog, causing quite a scene at royal dinners. Armadillos snort when they move around, imagine that!' he chuckled. It was the first time Malika had seen the widower's teeth. They were grey. He sighed, 'Ah, to live in romantic days of old!'

Mr Saeed's rejuvenation was even rarer than the antique. She listened like a novice to his anglicized Urdu, and to the unexpectedly dulcet lilt of his voice, imagining how different his household would be if it rang with it. Instead, once the payments were made and the dealer had left, Mr Saeed withdrew into his shell.

Now she tiptoed once more to the leather door of his study and rapped on it gently. Not surprisingly, no one answered. She turned the knob and peeped inside, conscious of invading his most dearly guarded space.

She could barely decipher his gaunt frame in a swivel chair behind which thick curtains draped a window. A slant of sunlight bounced off the studded armadillo that occupied at least a third of his desk. It was his only source of light as he wrote in the files where he kept records of his relics. She knew from her last time here, when she was hired, that the steps to his left led to the halls of the gallery. But otherwise, the objects in the room were indistinguishable. Since she was not permitted to clean it, dust settled everywhere in thick sheets. The combination of dirt and darkness made it impossible to guess the shape or colour of anything but the stuffed burrower and the prism of carmine about it. Her eye was drawn stubbornly back to the beast, dead and dazzling, as she spoke. 'I was wondering,' she cleared her throat, 'if you could spare a few seconds.'

He continued writing in his files.

Accustomed to his manner, she continued, 'My husband and I have both, by the grace of God, inherited a large sum of money.' She waited. He ceased scribbling but still did not look up. She continued, 'So my husband feels it unnecessary for me to continue working here.'

An echo of a voice, so unlike the one that had caressed a

dead beast, spoke from between the pages. 'I'll raise your salary.'

'You've already been very gracious,' the rubies danced in her eyes. 'I could never accept more.'

He impatiently brushed aside a layer of dust from before his eyes with the pencil in his cinereous fingers, as though it was she. 'My children need you.'

Malika sighed, 'So do mine.'

He dropped the pencil, and she realized that he too now stared at the armadillo. 'How can I persuade you to stay?'

The solitary diamond flashed ludicrously in the mammal's open snout. How painful that must have been, thought Malika, imagining some sharp instrument pierce her own tongue. She would be rendered a mute, locked within a prison of words like the Indian queen herself, showpiece to the British and later, leper to the nationalists. It was a miracle the relic had survived. A pity almost. For here was another toy Mr Saeed preferred over his own gilded children. If they were history, thought Malika, he would love them.

This speculation was not making her task easy. Was she to be like him, and abandon his children?

Mr Saeed burrowed into his files, eager to be alone again.

'Perhaps there is something,' she said at last. He might have nodded. 'I'll stay if my son is here with me. He won't get in your way. I also ask that we be allowed the afternoons off, after I've fed your children lunch and put them to sleep. When I stay till teatime it gets too late.'

He tapped his pencil thoughtfully, or irritably, then shrugged his shoulders. 'One more child won't make a difference. Saima can prepare the tea. Will that be all then?'

'Well,' Malika smiled coyly. 'On second thoughts I suppose we could always use a small raise . . . ?'

'It's settled,' he cut her off, and Malika knew her audience was over.

Chapter Ten

The night was so dark Mrs Masood feared she was going blind. She lay in bed, listening to Mr Masood breathing, smelling his rancid breath. A second odour enveloped her, a combination of wine, mustard and old age. It was her grandmother. Mrs Masood's fingers, terrified of what they might touch in the dark, remained glued beneath the covers. The old woman's tresses coiled around her own like snakes. Or perhaps they really were snakes. Tomorrow she must remember to string an onion and garlic-head under the bed to ward off the sah pina snakes that had followed her to the city. For now, she must survive the night.

With a degree of courage that surprised her, she sat up. The grandmother heaved too. She shut her eyes. Nothing could be worse than spending the night like this, sitting beside a figure whose breathing was now heard over her husband's, and whose position mirrored her own. Gingerly, in a gesture that was barely decipherable, she lifted her thumb. The foreign body did the same! 'Dadi,' she softly prayed. 'If it's you, please leave me.' There was a long-lasting sigh, like a punctured tyre, and the old woman collapsed into nothingness. But before Mrs Masood could breathe easy, another body inflated beside her. It touched her thumb with its own, as delicately as an insect extends a feeler. The scent of old age had gone, but that of mustard remained. It was Soomla. The churail held Mrs Masood's chin firmly in her cold fingers and pulled it sideways, forcing Mrs Masood to meet her walleyed. But when she turned there was nothing.

She rose from her bed and silently tiptoed outside. She pressed her chest against the corridor walls. The firmness was momentarily calming. She followed the walls to Laila's door.

Her daughter slept with the soft bedside lamp lit. It cast a welcoming peach colour over the lavender counterpane, like dawn on the sea. Laila slept on her side, her thick, black hair over her face. Mrs Masood listened to the girl's even breathing with relief. She could endure the wrath of Soomla if Laila was safe.

Facing Mrs Masood was the closet which contained some of the dowry. Mother and daughter had spent all year accumulating it. Some things were still in the process of being made. Mrs Masood knew she would have to cancel the orders to ensure payment to Soomla, who might well up the ante. Tears filled her eyes. She longed to load Laila with the gifts her own family had refused her. Laila was innocent, why should she suffer?

Dejectedly, she examined the long line of clothes hanging in the closet. There were embroidered silk ghararas, organza jackets, lace vests, sleek black tunics in tissue, velvet skirts, mirrored kameezes, French-knotted backless dresses, net pajamas, crocheted peshwazes and heavily embossed dupattas. Underneath lay rows of neatly arranged shoes, most of them still in boxes. Behind this was a large jewellery box. She opened it. It wasn't even half full yet. There was an emerald set, a string of pearls, ruby tops and a large diamond teeka that was to be worn at the wedding, for she had decided that every article worn on that day must be, if not white, then at least clear. There was also Laila's most prized possession: a designer necklace consisting of ornately-cut gilded leaves which overlapped each other so that, from a distance, it looked like one hefty sheet of gold. Laila favoured it over the traditional designs, since even her fiancé André recognized the artist's name. Mrs Masood knew she *ought* to love it, but secretly found it somewhat clumsy. Besides, though it contained only semiprecious stones, it had cost more than all the other jewels combined. It alone could protect their family against Soomla for the rest of their lives.

She sat at the edge of Laila's bed, brushing the girl's locks off her silken cheeks, the cheeks that drove her betrothed insane with passion. 'I'm sorry,' she whispered, 'but who knows how much more the churail will demand of me? She's threatened to destroy your marriage. I act in your interest. Will you ever understand?'

Necklace in hand, she kissed Laila goodnight and felt her way down the corridor again.

In her sweaty palms, the gilded leaves came alive. They fluttered out from between her fingers and circled the living room, settling in a neat line down the chir cabinet, beckoning Mrs Masood to open it. She obeyed, grabbing the first wine bottle in sight. The leaves dispersed once more, leading her to the gold divan.

As she sipped her wine, the leaves sprinkled gold dust over the sandalwood table. It alone became visible in the pitch blackness of the living room. Mrs Masood was forced to confront the table's resplendent beauty, forced to consider how her *minor* crime of cheating a poor man was resulting in such extreme disaster. The more she drank, the greater grew her conviction that the punishment did not merit the crime, and that had it been undiscovered by Soomla, Chaudry would never suffer as now she did.

But it was as though Soomla heard her remorseless thoughts, for she could suddenly smell the caseous odour of the churail's feet. Mrs Masood fought to reject her dissolute ideas. She made an excruciating effort to repent. But Soomla was here to stay. The frolicking leaves rose from Chaudry's table and hung around the invisible figure beside her, gradually bringing into view the inverted feet that dangled, golden and bodiless, close by. Mrs Masood trembled like a hunted pheasant and hastily swilled wine.

When next she looked around, the wall-to-wall print of Versailles was being smothered in a gold dust storm, illuminating the clipped shrubs that tapered at their tips like needles, the perfectly cropped grass, the irresistibly neat rows of roses—how she *loved* their orderliness—and the relaxed tourists walking arm-in-arm through it all, with hair powdered gold. It was paradise! Soomla's feet danced toward the print. Mrs Masood followed. The wall gave like water. In the gardens she was surrounded by scores of Soomla's offspring feet, swathed in gilded anklets and toe rings. They scrambled over Mrs Masood, pulling her gently onto the dew-swept grass. One pair proceeded to shampoo her hair with mustard, another fed her raspberries dipped in Grand Marnier, a third pitted grapes, and a fourth rubbed her loins with rosewater. She sank into a hypnotic sleep, dreaming of Camembert-scented feet.

Chapter Eleven

On the number fifteen minibus, Malika wrapped her arms around Momin's sparrow-like body and smiled proudly.

In the three weeks that he had been away from the loom, though Momin's bones remained misshapen, at least his cuts had grown scabs. He still wore henna to fool Chaudry, but Malika now looked upon the dye with a new perturbation. Whereas before it had been a symbol of Momin's bondage, now it spoke of his emancipation, as well as the price of it. Normally worn by brides and women in a festive spirit, the garish hue had become an ugly reminder of how she deceived her groom.

'That's Empress Market,' she whispered in his pixy ears, pointing at a mass of colourful shawls billowing in the dusty air. The bus was forced to decelerate. 'The Saeed children love to wander there,' she indicated a particularly fetid area of the bazaar. 'We'll all go together this Thursday. You'll see several varieties of birds, dogs and fish.' Momin absorbed her every word without answering. Malika paused, remembering the caged finches, tearful puppies and beady-eyed lobsters. She lost interest in telling him more about the market, and silently rubbed his tender earlobes. A water-carrier walked outside, crouching beneath the weight of his goatskin bag, which leaked from one corner. The man's dhoti was tied high above his knees. The veins of his emaciated legs bulged as though themselves about to tear.

With Momin beside her, the men of the bus left her alone. Though now a mere child, in later years he would be a man, replete with honour, memory and muscle. Malika humoured their foolishness, for in actuality it was she, not Momin or Chaudry, who could fight. She thought contentedly of her pact with Mrs Masood. She had not only secured a copious income, but as of this week, had also ensured that Mrs Masood would turn over her car and driver to Malika in the afternoons if she should so wish. Hence, in the free time Malika had won from Mr Saeed, she hoped to give Momin all the childhood things he had missed while at the factory.

The bus turned onto the wider M.A. Jinnah Road and accelerated with relief. There was less traffic, less noise, and a youthful wind ruffled the hair of the passengers. Malika watched Momin gaze with absolute stillness at an unfamiliar landscape. He rarely even blinked, so eager was he to hold each sight, to frame and preserve it in the as yet brittle recesses of his awakening life. Like the trees and flowers preparing for winter, he was cautious, self-absorbed and patiently awaited spring.

When they passed Jinnah's mausoleum he turned very slightly for another look at its pearly dome. 'We can go there later today if you want,' she said fondly, this time confident of being able to keep her promise. 'Don't you love the shimmering stone?'

He continued pursuing the ghost of the dome.

'In the sunlight it's translucent, like an eggshell.' She added thoughtfully, 'Like a myna's egg. There are many birds in the Mazar gardens. Your father and I once saw a nest with three pale and glossy eggs in the branches of a tree there.' Malika lost herself in Momin's imagination and continued, 'When we returned a few days later, they had hatched, and the mother was feeding the blind, furry chicks caterpillars. The babies had abnormally gigantic mouths. Pink inside. They opened and closed them at the same time.'

He stared ahead again, photographing the world with hungry eyes.

'There are luscious gardens surrounding the National Museum too,' Malika rattled excitedly, remembering a joyous day with Chaudry. 'It's not too far from here. Your father was always fascinated by the relics, though I never understood why. They looked like old toys.' She smiled, thinking of the awkwardly-cut clay figurines arranged in important-looking glass cases, each labelled in writing she could not read. Chaudry had excitedly drawn her attention to long stone objects, lingams he had called them, explaining they were replicas of the erect phallus the Indus Valley people worshipped. She had blushed uncontrollably, not expecting a husband to be so frank. He had teased her, saying the ancient people knew a thing or two.

She laughed secretly at her innocence, and a twinge of regret pierced her heart, for they had ceased enjoying excursions together ever since he threw their older sons out of the house. Instead, in bitter desperation, they had produced Faika. Now she and Momin pursued their own happiness, retracing older ones, and Chaudry could never know.

'You'll learn all about the civilization in school,' Malika

continued, determined not to feel guilty. 'Maybe we can make a trip to Mohenjo-daro so you can see the ruins.'

Momin smiled. It was his first gesture of acquiescence. She squeezed and smothered him with kisses. He yielded, limp as a kitten.

'My son!' she whispered, choking with love. 'I told you I'd rescue you from the factory. I told you I'd send you to school. Trust me now?'

He blinked, speechless.

They were approaching the Sports Complex. Malika asked, 'Tell me, what is it you'd like to see most?'

But Momin could not yet say what there was to see. His eyes sought hers for direction. She smothered him again, wanting nothing more than for him to need, adore and own her. It was the least she could expect for setting him free.

The bus stalled at their stop and the men made way for them to exit unharmed.

Chapter Twelve

Often Mr Masood returned home with the French men without notifying his wife in advance. Though they never stayed for dinner, the guests sat around the living room for hours, oblivious that others wished to dine. Tonight, the orbicular Chauclet, 'so as not to trouble the Madame', had brought his own wine. Rubbing his pudgy fingers fondly over each bottle, he joked that he merely followed the Pakistani custom of the groom's family offering gifts to the bride's.

Mrs Masood thanked him profusely, for it meant the cabinet's missing loot would remain undiscovered. At least for now.

As they drank, M. Didier underwent his characteristic transformation: from predator-before-attack, to semi-preened duckling, to sated predator. It was in the last phase, when others grew dopey, that he began a hunt of a nature that was neither urgent nor hungry, but cool and detached. Of Mrs Masood he demanded black coffee, to be made with his coffee beans in his coffee maker, both of which he diligently carried with him on each visit. Of Mr Masood he claimed more sales, more profits and fewer costs, to which the owner druggedly consented.

When she was not preparing the coffee, Mrs Masood lounged with the men. But she barely recognized her surroundings. Her fingers crept like crabs on her dupatta, her tongue raged like a tumour, and under her breath she prayed that the guests would depart soon so her husband would eat and sleep, and she could sip the remaining wine. For djinns tore her insides furiously when she was dry, like angry rats fighting for crumbs. In the three weeks since the churail Soomla's first visit, Mrs Masood had discovered that wine alone could put them to sleep. Then her tongue, though it never again offered her the nectarous pleasures of her first drops, at least numbed.

Till the men left, however, she was dutiful, thirsty and had an explosive headache.

M. Chauclet chatted excitedly about tapenade, an olive and anchovy paste of southern France that had been served at every wedding in his family for generations. Mr Masood mumbled doltishly that he would do his best. Mrs Masood listened. Their words sounded from an unknown corner of the universe, like the voices of early morning before she was fully awake. She sought her husband as though he were a compass, but he flipped incongruously, and instead of a commanding businessman with a stubborn head of wooly hair, she saw a sluggish man, grey and wrinkled, nodding in perpetual agreement like an elephant. She watched breathlessly, eyes narrowed, convinced that the cabinet director and his friend were poisoning him.

'Tomorrow I will bring for you a priceless wine, from the Domaine de Trevallon, north of Aix,' M. Chauclet sighed, and brushed away a tear from one corner of his puffy eyes.

Mrs Masood winced at the gesture, whereby, one by one, the Frenchman's stubby fingers plucked out the features of his bloated face. He popped them in the pink, salivating space of his enormous mouth and ground them with his steely jaws in her ear. No one protested.

The featureless Chauclet continued, 'But then we must have ramekins, made only with quail eggs. Oh,' he brushed his bone-white face where a tear would have grown, and like a magician pulling a dove from a silken handkerchief, a third eye emerged, 'you simply *must* have quail in this country?' He swallowed the fresh eye. Mrs Masood heard it crack, and yolk spilled like wine from hidden lips.

'Oh yes,' belched Mr Masood. 'We consider it a delicacy ourselves . . . '

'How foolish you are, Ronald,' M. Didier interrupted, swinging his immense legs reproachfully. 'Encouraging them to duplicate our ways in this land. How can they possibly succeed? Wasn't dinner the other night evidence enough? And what is this absurd monstrosity?' He flapped his vulture's wings at the print of Versailles in the living room.' And there,' he leaned toward the French windows. 'What indeed are you hoping to achieve *there*?'

Everyone stared blankly out of the windows, where the gardeners had commenced transplanting the Christmas topiary. The men should have left hours ago. But tonight a few had stayed on as the plants were misbehaving. Mrs Masood shook her head to clear the picture before her eyes, but it only grew muddier. In the floodlit mass of falling boxwood needles stood lopsided images that in no way resembled the wall-to-wall print of the palace gardens, nor of the drawings she had made when inspired by *All The World Loves France*. On paper, the angels she drew had stood on tiptoe, waving delicate wands and smiling blissfully beneath protective halos. But in life, their dainty legs stuck together and wobbled like a cripple's. In fact, their feet turned backwards. The halos, instead of hovering luminously, collapsed over their eyes like blindfolds. She counted urgently, one, two, three . . . that was all she had asked for, believing the number significant to Christians. But there were thirteen in a circle. While the gardeners struggled to plant them, each figure twisted and turned as though struck by a bullet, and the wands waved haphazardly away from their bodies. In the centre, instead of a reindeer, stooped something resembling a camel. It was led by a Santa Claus who was neither fat nor jolly but shrivelled and with boxwood needles piercing his eyes like hot desert sand.

A hollow laugh sounded from the blank-faced Chauclet, 'Mon Dieu!'

'Madame . . . ' a nettled M. Didier turned to Mrs Masood. In an effort at composure, he stirred his dark coffee while Mrs Masood watched, eagerly awaiting the rest of the sentence. He continued stirring, as though re-brewing it. Steam rose from between his fingers and the liquid thickened. A familiar smell drifted through the room.

Mrs Masood remembered how her grandmother had described the dense smell of the room the churail had lured her grandfather and uncle into. 'The odour was strongest near the carpenter's table . . . ' Her grandmother had said, while an aunt matted mustard oil into the old woman's silvery head.

M. Didier stirred the mixture with hooked talons, testing its consistency by pulling out a claw that glistened with an ever-changing brew, first tar black, then mud brown, then red. He licked himself clean and continued stirring, occasionally spilling a drop or two in the vines of the sandalwood table.

Mrs Masood's fingers raced fearfully under her dupatta. She contemplated getting a sponge to clean up the mess.

'Ahem,' began M. Didier, disdainfully looking away from Mrs Masood, toward her perpetually nodding husband. 'In the seventeenth and eighteenth centuries, France produced pile-woven carpets based on Eastern techniques, and perfected them. It's a tragedy of the East. When the West takes from it, the West thrives. But when it takes from the West, the East makes a monkey of itself.' Then he tossed back his drink, coffee cup and all, and looked at Mrs Masood with a china handle sticking like a nose ring from his beak. 'Savonnerie,' he continued, 'was the name of the weaving centre. It was a favourite of King Louis XIV. His palace still exhibits the woven treasures. We have preserved them as flawlessly as we imitated them.' He regurgitated and once more swallowed the china cup, flapping his arms again at the garden. 'How far you are from understanding!'

She was speechless. M. Chauclet was saying something about pork pâté. Mr Masood nodded. Outside the gardeners struggled to keep the camel jockey on the camel, and the camel on his feet. Struck by more bullets, the angels jerked violently, their wands quavering toward the centre of the circle. There stood the animal so like Sirkash, the self-satisfied camel of her Cholistani past. Or was it her present?

Mrs Masood struggled to place herself in time but the effort was stultifying. She forced herself to sit upright, unable to contain the surge of hatred she felt for Sirkash. He spent his days lolling moodily on the dunes, nibbling the lana plant he so adored. He worked only for her grandmother, who lovingly braided his tail and mane, hennaed his hide and sewed an intricate mesh of beads and shells to his harness. The shells were from the desert itself; the Indus had once coursed through there. Astride Sirkash, the grandmother became the tallest creature of the desert. It was said that her powers heightened from that position, so she could see the globe and smell the seasons. That was how her family always knew when to move and where to find the sweetest wells, while others waited in vain for rain.

Many men tried to buy the animal, but her grandmother merely laughed her dry, gritty laugh singing, 'One man's blessing is another man's curse!' A few attempted theft. Sirkash dealt with them in his characteristically unpredictable way: swiftly crushing their skulls in his jaws, or allowing them to mount and riding placidly to the farthest away dune, where then he vanished without a footprint to guide them back. 'Learn from him, child!' Her grandmother would say. 'The animal is fearless and proud, these are the qualities you need to survive. But instead,' she would sigh knowingly, 'your brain is scrambled. What will become of you?'

The gardeners pushed and heaved, but they succeeded only in stripping off the boxwood needles that weighted Sirkash. As the creature grew increasingly spare he smiled with greater disdain.

'Failure!' The angels outside pointed their wands accusingly toward the living room, at Mrs Masood, and chimed in a chorus, 'We warned you!'

Santa Claus slid off the camel's triangular hump and shook his fist furiously at her, sending a torrent of needles through the air till there was nothing left of his arm but the wire that was meant to hold it. And then the rest of him shed. He became a metal skeleton poking haphazardly in the air. He cursed viciously as he tripped and stumbled out of the gate. Then her grandmother tossed her wand far into the sky and leaped onto the camel's back. The animal rose. Both had lost most of their leaves. Coils of wire burned red in the sun, like bald skin, as they rode steadily out of the garden, followed by all but one of the angels.

M. Didier cleared his throat and his nose ring vibrated. He spoke, but Mrs Masood could not understand his words. She heard herself speak with a foreign voice in a foreign tongue, 'Versailles'. An echo of laughter sifted through her brain. She tried to identify where it came from. It could be the outside world, where M. Didier circled her with scorn, and Chauclet was an O with only air passing through him, blowing an infinitesimal menu. Or it could be from inside her, where djinns nipped in hunger. Or the world beyond the outside world, a place that only her grandmother could see, as she rode on Sirkash.

And where, she wondered, did her garden go? The more she sought to tame it, the wilder it grew, each sculpted bush shrinking from her grasp like her self-control. She could no longer hear the sprinklers whipping in unison.

Outside, the last of the angels, the thirteenth, tried to wriggle loose. Her blindfold fell to her neck like a noose. Mrs Masood dimly recognized first herself, then Laila, then a woman who resembled them both. 'Mother!' She heard herself cry in a foreign voice with a foreign tongue. The gardeners wrapped the body tightly in cable so it would stay.

Chapter Thirteen

While Malika spent the mornings inside Mr Saeed's old home, Momin loitered through its sprawling, deserted grounds. She watched him from the kitchen window, prowling with hands behind his back to conceal their deformity.

Besides the occasional visits from the doddering doorman who was also the gardener, but who preferred to tend the carport, Momin had all three acres of the property to himself. He claimed it in quiet ceremony, walking meditatively on little feet ensconced in new white tennis shoes that he cleaned daily to keep fresh for the school he would attend in two months. Sometimes he lay supine on the steps of the aging amphitheatre, listening to its silence, gazing at the pariah kites above. On other days he watered and weeded the large, sunken rectangle immediately beneath Mr Saeed's balcony, where once, the old gardener told him, the late Mrs Saeed had grown roses.

On her trips to the Masood household, Malika would

consult the handsome gardener, and return to Momin with cuttings and instructions on how to root them. He worked patiently in the sunken garden, waiting to see what 'roses' were. Above him lurked the shadow of Mr Saeed, his worn dressing gown swooping around him like wings. Momin responded with curiosity and awe, and a few times Malika even heard him attempt a conversation with the wings: 'My name's Momin. And yours?' But they never answered. Momin would casually resume work, unruffled by the phantom above.

But around the Saeed children his budding confidence wavered, and the older, timid self threatened to consume him. To disguise this, he adopted an inimical demeanour, as if challenging the children to disturb his peace. He was especially wary of Faisal, who fiercely demanded Malika's attention. He watched icily while she propped him on her lap, though he was *older* than him, and cooed the boy through lunch. When Faisal accepted milk in a glass instead of a bottle, and she kissed his roseate cheeks, Momin would turn the other way as though his own had been slapped.

For his part, now that Momin was there, Faisal often drank from a glass. It kept Malika's focus on him. If she attended instead to Momin, he cried. And she, afraid that Mr Saeed would banish Momin from a house that, at least in the mornings, gave him three acres of utmost joy, plus free meat and milk, quickly returned to the surrogate son. Faisal, sensing victory, gradually prevented her from even talking to Momin in his presence.

Fazeel, distant as ever, barely even noticed Momin. And Saima responded in her characteristically mercurial way, sometimes with friendly chatter, at others with venom. She loved to cajole Momin into mimicking her principal Mr Brown's children. 'They talk to foolishly,' she would say. 'You try it.' She would stick a pencil between his teeth, forcing him to speak without dropping it. When he froze with fright she would smother him with kisses exclaiming, 'I'm so glad you're not like them,' and prop him on her lap like Malika did Faisal.

On unluckier days, her affection turned acrid.

One day she returned from school furious with her best friend Naz. She had thrown a party without her. As always happened when she was incensed, Saima screamed in vain at an absent father. Later, she burst into the kitchen, panting. Fazeel hurried to his toy army. Faisal sucked vigorously on his milk bottle and a trembling Momin, with nowhere to hide, clenched a disfigured fist. In a chilling voice Saima began, 'And how is Midget Momin today?'

Momin feigned deafness. Malika felt his heart collide into hers.

'Do you have a middle name?' Her large chestnut eyes narrowed behind square spectacles with black frames heavy like stratocumulus. 'Could it be Mute? Are you Midget Mute Momin? Or perhaps Mulish? Myopic? Or, it must be, Mousy, like my darling father! No? Multiped? A Mutant version of your bizarre Mother and her Martian feet?' Saima was blessed with the capacity to enunciate particularly well when enraged.

Though Malika tried, her feet would not be reined. Under the table, they writhed in apoplectic fury while Saima watched disgustedly. No more, Malika thought to herself. Why should I feel responsible for the widower's bratty children? Tomorrow we'll leave. And some day, once he gets his diploma, Momin will be accomplished enough to have his own three acres, in his own palace. She looked at her son consolingly but Faisal was still in her lap, clinging greedily, and Momin ignored them all. He studied the bright hands of Woody Woodpecker waving beckoningly around the clock above them. At two o'clock, a smaller bird would poke out of its nest. At three the children would be fast asleep and she and Momin could leave. Mrs Masood's car would be waiting for them.

'Dammit!' Saima slammed her plate. Shards of beef and china flowered their hair. 'Why is everyone in this house so bloody dead!' She raced upstairs and all of them, including Baby Woodpecker, breathed a sigh of relief.

The next morning, Momin marked every inch of his space in an even slower, statelier gait. He noticed a lizard had made a fresh nest in the earth. To it he conceded a boundary. He saw where the moles hid. They asked him to build a rockery for they needed walls. He resolved to make a pond, a small one, enough to make the dragonflies stay, for he loved their papery, pastel-coloured wings, stiff as blades. Malika knew they could not leave.

Still, she searched desperately for a chance to explain her relationship with the Saeed children, so he could understand it centred around him. When they were alone, she fed him all kinds of treats: sweet lassi, dazzling jalebis, Multani halwa and kulfi. She even offered him a flask to carry with him to the gardens, filled with his favourite drink, Pepsi. When he returned to the kitchen, she showered him with compliments on the garden, eager for confidences. But Momin never again smiled at her trustingly, as he had that first time on the bus.

That day however he took regular breaks from the grounds to visit her in the kitchen. He fluttered quietly beside her, as though expecting more. She was too nervous to respond flatly: 'I'm forced to ignore you in Faisal's presence because . . .' He was so fragile, so young. Instead, she chattered about nothing, avoiding his eyes, for they cut through her charade.

Around one o'clock, while Malika fried chapli kebabs, Momin surprised her by offering to lay the table. Until now, he had wanted nothing to do with any ritual that involved the children. She keenly consented.

He neatly arranged the tablemats, and asked, 'Why won't the shadow on the balcony speak?'

Malika's heart raced: finally, an opportunity to explain herself. She sat at the table and answered, 'The shadow belongs to Mr Saeed. His silence is caused by the death of his wife. He suffers a terrible pain.' She paused, meticulously arranging the words she wished to speak next in her brain.

Momin piled the plates up and put the knives where the forks had been, and the spoons in place of the knives. Then he jumbled them up and started over.

'You see,' Malika gently pulled him toward her, 'his poor children don't have a mother like you do.'

He regarded her thoughtfully. 'They have a father.'

She coughed awkwardly. Was he implying that he did not have a father, or even a mother? Hastily, she changed the subject. 'Did you drink the Pepsi?'

He studied her.

She rose to fry onions, shuddering at how old her son had become. A protracted silence drew more years between them.

Finally, he helped himself to a glass of orange juice and returned to her side. 'Yes, I did. And I saw shiny, black birds with colourful dots on their wings pecking at the grass.'

She smiled. 'They're called starlings. Because the dots shimmer in the dark like stars.'

Recognition flooded his face. 'Then is that why Mr Saeed is called the Crow, because of his black cloak?'

'Exactly!' she played along happily. 'That's how the neighbours know him.'

The clock chimed to indicate the children had to be brought home from school. Their time alone here had ended. She searched his eyes for disappointment. 'Don't forget once the children are asleep, we can go wherever you want,' she reminded him gently.

Momin flapped his arms and floated out of the kitchen shrieking, 'I'm a crow! I'm a crow!'

That afternoon, Saima bubbled with affection for Momin. She fed him the tenderest botis, plumpest chicken legs, and from her knapsack produced Pepsi, in a can! After lunch, she led him to her room, where a fan whizzed soporifically, and candy-coloured books dappled a soothing navy-blue carpet. Saima settled in the centre, crossed her naked, spindly legs and pulled Momin down beside her. 'Choose,' she tilted her head to indicate the books. Heavy, nut-brown hair draped her shoulders like a sheet of silk.

Momin stared, wide-eyed and open-mouthed. Slowly, his hand came out from its customary position at his back. It lingered uncertainly about her hair while his gaze turned from the glittery books to her undulating tresses and back to the books.

'Hasn't anyone ever read you a story?'

He shook his head.

Malika frowned, both at her own illiteracy and Saima's deliberate reference to it.

'Oh you poor boy!' she cuddled him. Her hair tickled his face. 'I read Faisal a tale every night. He's a spoiled brat!'

Faisal, still in Malika's lap, howled. Malika caressed his cheek. He hushed, but watched the other two. So did Malika.

'Let's see now,' Saima continued, 'How about *Tom Thumb?*'

Momin studied the picture of a tiny boy, dressed in a cap of grass and shirt of cobwebs, surrounded by grotesque giants with thirsty eyes. He nodded.

She began, 'Once upon a time, a peasant couple who longed for a child visited a witch who knew all the secrets of nature. She granted them their wish, a thumb-sized creature who could only have the softest and purest materials brush his tender skin . . .'

Momin sank into the curve of Saima's supple arm and cautiously touched her hair.

'He slept in a pomegranate rind, under an eighth of his mother's sheer, white chiffon dupatta. She would shake it under the fan so it blew in delicate waves, and he fell asleep watching silken hills turn to vapour-thin cups. At night his dreams were sweet. Creatures just like himself caressed a wind cloth as it breathed around them. Their chins nudged it to shape, turning cups into domes that fit their cheeks. They were silkworms spinning a cocoon that only they could see, and that would protect them forever.'

She turned the page, 'But in real life Tom Thumb was destined for adventure, and it was not long before the delicate mist of his mother's dupatta whispered change. One day he found himself riding in the beak of a damp and restless crow. The feathered beast, deciding little Tommy was not what she wanted, threw him down a chimney. In a pratfall he landed in the House of Big People. Look,' Saima pointed to a picture of Tom Thumb rubbing his sore bottom. She read the caption, 'The Big People tore off his finery, including the good luck dori he wore around his neck, made from two hairs of his mother's eyebrows.'

Momin, Malika and Faisal peeped eagerly inside the book. Saima clasped Momin like a bear does her cub. 'Shall I go on?'

He nodded again.

'The ogres stuffed Tom Thumb in a dress of wood, which sawed his bones to powder. He became an all-purpose tool around the house—bait for mice and rats, a broom to sweep out dirt, and a key to open locks. They jabbed him between their teeth like a toothpick, smothering him with their odious breath. They turned him into a bootjack. The stench of their socks sent him doubling over in a coughing fit, causing the wooden dress to crush him further. They twirled him in their ears and ordered, "Scratch!" and he scooped out mountains of sticky, yellow muck with naked fingers.

'Soon poor Tommy developed hideous warts all over his minor frame. If his mother were to see him now, she would never know him. He cried in vain for her. Then he took matters into his own hands. The next time a giant used him as a toothpick, he slid down his lichened gullet and fell plum into a mass of wet blubber. He slid from one fatty deposit to another. The Big Person, sickened by the movement in his belly, ran to the topmost storey of his comfy abode and vomited far into the Arabian Sea.

'Tom Thumb's wooden dress kept him afloat, till an Unlucky Fisherman found him in his net. The sea had cleansed Tommy's wounds and salty scabs covered his tender flesh like scales. The old man had never seen the likes of such a fish before. He rapped on its shell and declared it a rare thing, the last of its kind, a piece of history. Tom Thumb cried, "Set me free!" But the fisherman could not hear him, and seeing the creature's legs wriggle, tied Tommy to the end of a fish line as bait. That day, and every day after, he returned home with a tremendous catch. Soon he became known as the Lucky Fisherman.

'After his long mornings at sea, the Lucky Fisherman put his bait in the sun to dry and at night fed it moths and ants. But the dress never dried entirely and Tommy grew increasingly unhappy in its heavy, sea-soaked darkness, which swelled to resemble the hump of some exotic Unknown. When the fisherman showed him off to the villagers, they cried, "A worm!" Or, "a snail!" Or, "a turtle!" The elders swore they had seen something like it before, in a desert long ago. No one guessed he was just a boy with a bad cold.

'One day, while Tommy drifted in the sea attracting many curious fish, he darted inside the jaws of an unusually large minnow. It snipped the fish line with fierce teeth and escaped the Lucky Fisherman's net. It was very watery inside the minnow. Tom Thumb shivered and sneezed and fell into a delirious sleep. His dress crumbled off and he felt himself sinking. Then he heard a low, plaintive song that seemed to carry him back in time—or maybe forward. He ceased feeling cold, and the memory of his mother burst like a bubble. He entered a place of immense vitreous darkness filled with the wail of the sea. He had returned to the lair of the witch, the same one who had brought him to Earth.

'"It's as I suspected," the wise magician said. "The Big People want you only to satisfy their own greed." And then she cast a spell on the land, whereby every man and woman turned sterile.

'At last Tom Thumb had a good long rest.'

Saima put down the book and pulled Momin's fingers from off her hair. 'Did you like that, you poor, twisted, little imp?'

Momin instantly hid his hands.

Saima smiled amusedly, 'Don't be so timid. It'll amount to nothing. Now, it's way past our naptime. If I feel like it, tomorrow I'll read you another tale.'

Chapter Fourteen

At night Mrs Masood returned to the garden. In her hands, she carried a Merlot that M. Chauclet had brought on his last visit. Or perhaps it was the time before.

Beneath a white, wintry moon the thirteenth angel's hair covered in frost. Mrs Masood swilled the great French wine and watched the angel, tangled in twine, age in front of her. In the fogginess of her mind she remembered a picture seen in a book long ago. It may have been the one with scenes from Versailles. A fire crackled in someone's wooden cabin, its glare burning red on the faces of the children huddled before it. Behind them was a French window. Outside a milky sky blew masses of tissue paper around a figure wrapped in white robes, whose eyes flashed candent. The caption had read, 'Un enfant de neige'. She looked it up: a snowchild. Mrs Masood could not quite decide whether the longing in her eyes was chaste or lewd.

Now she lay on the lawn carpeted with boxwood needles

and dew, and contemplated the solitary angel. The Snow Angel, she would call her, with a prickly, imprisoned body turning to hoar. The Snow Angel's teeth chattered in the late night air, but Mrs Masood felt snug. She drifted asleep.

In her dreams she heard nails hammer, and then a familiar voice say, 'The bed is made.' Her grandmother pushed her to a young groom. He stepped aside so she could prostrate herself for him. The bed was white and wispy like milkweed. 'Finer than your hair,' the same familiar voice said.

They tossed all night, husband and wife, he breathing milkweed follicles on her skin, she scratching. Glass tinkled, as when wind blows through a chandelier. He slept and the bed grew cold. She realized it was not glass she was hearing, but icicles tapping lightly against each other as they honed her flesh. Her teeth chattered. Beside her snored the grandmother. She yearned to curl into the aged woman's rustic back, to feel the ice break and flow like a river. But when the woman turned she was the churail Soomla. Soomla bounced on her chest, feet thrashing like a curse, pumping out her blood. Mrs Masood was transformed into a mere block of ice. M. Didier appeared with an axe. He hacked her into neat squares and dropped her in his drink. There she melted.

Chapter Fifteen

Reluctantly, Momin followed Malika into Mrs Masood's copper-hued Honda Saloon. She knew he was thinking of Saima, but swallowed her pride and delved once more for strength. 'I'm sorry,' she pressed his cheeks, flushed from the slap.

He stared vacantly around him. There was none of the wonder of his first drive. When they passed Tariq Road, Malika wanted to halt and buy him a newspaper conical of roasted chanaas, to watch him scrape off the husk and pop one hot golden ball after another into his tiny mouth. She wanted him to smell the pine nuts, and wander through the closet-tight maze of jalebi-coloured bracelets, rain-washed books and bolts of cotton. She wanted him to feel the energy of the myriad others who inhabited Karachi, and who survived it. But looking through his eyes she saw only bone-dry kittens, roiling potholes, and children who begged in the cradle.

It was time to get out of the city. 'Haleji Lake!' she ordered the well-groomed driver. She had promised to take Momin there a year ago. She never dreamed it would happen like this. Her temples throbbed with words she longed to speak: don't waste your love on Saima. But she bit her tongue and settled resignedly into the rhythm of the vehicle as it sped across the whirligig jungle, toward the highway. Eventually Malika was able to reflect upon the day.

Since *Tom Thumb*, Saima had been reading Momin stories every afternoon. Aside from the garden, it seemed there was nothing he cultivated more single-mindedly than her affection. He rejected the afternoon outings with Malika, choosing to stay behind even when she worked at Mrs Masood's. Saima had welcomed him. She said he brightened her days, and would he please wait at the front door for her when she came home from school? He would stand there, from the minute Malika left to pick up the children until they returned, an hour later.

But today, the malevolent itch that periodically irked Saima resurfaced. Malika had seen the change in the car. Saima had pulled off her school tie from around her throat and proceeded to knot its length, singing rancorously: 'This one's for you, Omar, and this one for *you* (she gave no name). This for Ama and this for Abu. This for Fazeel, this Faisal, and this for Mr Brown the arsehole. These are his kids, this his wife, and this his snotty pretentious life . . . '

When there were no more knots to fasten, she rolled the tie in a ball and flung it out at a taxi-driver. It hit his eye. She giggled. He said, 'Cunt.' She unleashed a string of curses. Malika plugged Faisal's ears. Their own driver, a lean old man whom they called simply Baba, like the doorman, shook his head and muttered, 'God protect us.' The taxi-driver followed them. Baba begged the man to leave.

'No begging; lead him to the house!' Saima rose to the occasion. 'Let Abu handle him!'

The taxi-driver leaned out his window, spat in her face and pulled away. By the time they reached the driveway Saima's wrath was sulphurous. Malika tried to warn Momin, but Saima was first through the door, where he was obediently stationed.

Her eyes narrowed spitefully, 'I'm sick of you following me about like a lovesick poodle!'

Momin stayed glued.

'Go on,' she snapped, 'scat!'

He was rooted.

Then she drew closer, and closer. The dense frames of her spectacles threatened to clap like thunder, her silken hair shimmered like the wings of a gigantic cockroach. He ran. She chased him, laughing, 'Now you know what it's like to be followed! You pathetic coward. You're just like the others!'

Malika scooped him in her arms and raced outside.

He kicked in protest, 'Take me back!'

She breathed heavily, 'The one time I want you to be quiet you won't shut up!'

He beat her chest with his crooked fists. She slapped him. When they reached Mrs Masood's car, she put him down and cried, 'Do what you want!'

They were alone at Haleji Lake. The water lapped gently against the embankment. Malika hoisted Momin onto it. He watched wood ducks dive headlong into the cool depths that were increasingly unable to feed Karachi. The ducks paddled noisily, quacked and drifted effortlessly on. The wet feathers of their buttocks curled fashionably atop their backs.

'Look there,' Malika pointed to a kingfisher diving for food. It ascended and perched on a willow branch, proudly displaying a silvery fish that squirmed in its beak.

'Do you think he's watching us?' she asked.

Momin regarded the cold tapering eyes, the strong pointed beak inflicting slow death. 'Yes,' he decided.

They stared at the bird in silence, Malika awestruck by his kingly control, Momin engrossed in the muscular neck and sienna breast band, the crest slicked back to accentuate the regal head. Then his attention switched to a pair of skinny legs swinging upward from the deep dark lake. They were his own. He unlaced his shoes, peeled off the socks, and dipped his naked feet inside. The reflection broke. He lifted his feet. It reappeared. Then it was rumpled by a small black fish with O-shaped lips. Before he could touch it the fish bolted, evanescent as a ghost.

'Do you like it here?' Malika pleaded.

When Momin nodded, it was not with excitement but resignation. She watched him draw circles in the water with his toes, peering past the ripples for fish. The creatures resurfaced, but always darted aside in time.

He was content, thought Malika. At least for now. But what he wanted was to be enamored She had wanted the power to draw the arrow, to choose what he should love. She suspected that this was not a mother's prerogative. Only in the wilderness could one creature exert such force on another. She watched the kingfisher mercilessly hold the fish in his beak. Your life is entirely in my hands, his steely eyes gloated. Malika felt no sorrow for the fish, nor indignation for the bird. But if they had been human?

She thought of Saima, Shafiq and Mrs Masood. Were they kingfishers or fish? And to which category did she belong? She thought of her trips to Mrs Masood's. At Malika's word, she downed the poison of the chir cabinet and lapsed into tedious chatter about her life in Cholistan, Laila, her husband. As though Malika cared. Then she would cry for water. Malika refused her. She imagined Mrs Masood's desiccated face in place of the fish below. It hung just beneath the lake's surface, unable to rise, unable to drown.

She felt no sorrow for it.

'Next time we should bring food,' she smiled at Momin, who had also befriended the loons and coots. He refused to breathe a word.

In her mind she formulated words to him: Saima isn't all bad, I suppose, but be cautious. Don't be gullible like your father. Build walls from people like her, not from me. Are the moles happier now? Maybe you could have a duck pond at the house. I know a gardener who could help. How lovely your shoes look. In another six weeks you'll be wearing them to school...

Though her eyes beheld the same landscape, suddenly her brain registered a difference. From the way Momin's mouth fell open she understood his instinct knew it too. A rush of wind, and swooping majestically before them was a great blue heron. Together they watched its flight, eagerly recording how it carried its curvaceous neck and dainty legs, how the long black feather tapering upward from its eyes sliced the wind. When it vanished, a nightmarish stillness descended on the lake. Malika found herself yearning for the creature's return, as though it alone could bridge the gap between herself and Momin. She waited. But like all things numinous, the heron would not appear when called.

The next day Saima returned home penitent. A new tie hung incisively down the centre of her starched shirt like a blade of honour; she would have hers back. After lunch she read Momin *The Boy Who Talked To Trees* till long after the siesta hour.

Fazeel and Faisal fell asleep. Malika sat reluctantly on the navy-blue carpet, listening to Saima sow wild fancies in the thirsty, freshly tilled earth of Momin's mind.

'This boy's just like you!' Saima tickled his slightly protruding tummy. 'Obsessed with flowers and plants.'

He's not like him, Malika frowned: *that* boy runs away from home.

She had hoped to take another trip into Sindh this afternoon, this time to the marshy Mancher Lake, north of Haleji. The lake was near the ancient town of Sehwan Sharif, where her family had lived for generations, before her great-grandfather finally moved to the city. She herself had never seen the swamp village, famed for its pottery, poetry and mystics. Unlike Chaudry, Malika rarely contemplated her family's past. She had no time. But now, while attempting to ground Momin in a safe present, she wondered if she shouldn't instill in him a little family pride?

Her plan had been ill fated. First Mrs Masood's driver had declared that the trip was too long for an afternoon, it would take the entire day. Besides, he had said in his customarily stiff manner, going that deep into the interior of the province was especially unsafe for a woman. His leaden eyes, Malika had thought, were definitely of the kingfisher order.

Then, to her horror, before she left to pick up the children, Momin planted himself in front of the door for Saima. 'But don't you remember yesterday?' Malika could not resist asking. He kept standing.

Finally, Saima had been in an exuberant mood and that was the end of that.

The story was nearly over. Saima described in great detail—more detail than could have been in the tale itself,

119

Malika was sure—the boy's mother's distress when she reads his parting letter, requesting that no one follow him. She shut the book and there was a moment's silence. Malika hoped it meant naptime. But Saima steered Momin into the TV room and placed all of Faisal's cartoon videos at his disposal. He chose the *Loony Toons*.

The breezy, capacious room was littered with stuffed pink panthers, plastic rattlesnakes, a toy piano, cymbals and myriad other objects with which the children entertained themselves on weekends and evenings, when Malika was away. It was immediately beneath Mr Saeed's room, so it opened onto Momin's sunken garden. She could not have chosen a more desired location. In one sweep Momin embraced both his loves: Saima and the roses.

They dived into a beanbag and rooted for Tweety to outwit Sylvester, which the little bird did, over and over, leaving Malika alone with her puzzle of Haleji Lake: who was the kingfisher and who the fish?

Part Three:
Lying in the Bed We Made

Chapter Sixteen

The carpenter Chaudry had lost weight since last winter, Malika observed one Friday. Last year's sweater, already a 'small', hung loose on him. He raved inside it, nibbling at himself to feed the wedding bed. Since Mrs Masood's payment of the deposit, he had become even more consumed by the project, often returning to it after dinner as if to pay his own debts.

Now it was Malika and Chaudry, not Malika and Momin, who rarely spent time together. Even the hours they did have—dinner during the week, lunch on Fridays—had changed. He no longer sculpted morsels for her mouth, musing over them till they were bite-size perfect. He did not ask for 'tricks'. Nor did he retell stories of his carpentry past. He was distracted, sullen almost. Malika feared he sniffed her conspiracy.

Today he coughed fiercely into the sweater, annoyed that the fit interfered with his favourite part of the work: the headboard. 'Watch carefully,' he ordered Momin, who still spent every Friday learning the craft.

Chaudry held the wood in place with a vice, so it rested in his lap like a sarod. In the past, he had held Malika this way. When he smelt the deodar's wild aroma and marvelled at its reddish hue, she remembered how he had inhaled her mustard-scented hair and indulged in its darkness. And when he carved the wood with a chisel he listened, as if the cedar sang, guiding him over its surface the way she had led him across her body with whimpers of encouragement.

Momin held his head in his hands, visibly bored. While at the factory, he had never had the courage to slouch at his father's art. He had sat upright, timid and obedient. Now in his sloppiness lurked an irony, thought Malika, as though he believed that if his father turned him out of the house like his brothers, he could run to Saima.

Malika despaired of Momin's naïveté. He was just like his father.

She had on the stove their weekly mutton korma and palau lunch and sat on the children's charpoi, finally mending the torn quilt. The drape between the store and the bedroom-kitchen was in the washtub outside, allowing her to witness, from her place on the bed, the action of her family.

She had flirted with the idea of buying a new quilt. But Chaudry had been impatient with the changes around the house.

'Unnecessary,' he had scowled at the rug and curtains, while, after noticing Momin's new tennis shoes and sweater, he accused her of squandering. 'And where is all this coming from?' he had suddenly thought to ask.

'Mr Saeed increased my salary,' she answered truthfully.

'Why did you accept? He already pays plenty.'

'He insisted.' Was this a lie? She paused, then added a

blatant one, 'He gives all his employees a raise every three years.'

Chaudry clicked his tongue petulantly, 'And you waste it on such inanities when you too could contribute to your daughter's future. Why do men alone understand the worth of saving for tomorrow?'

She had hated him then, for while he talked of saving it was she who built up their nest egg.

Now she re-stuffed the old quilt and sealed it with tight, punitive stitches.

Chaudry wiped his chisel on a leather apron and suddenly challenged Momin. 'How many knots did you tie yesterday?'

Malika tensed. She cracked her toes praying, please God, give the boy the wisdom to lie.

Momin offered his father a supremely indifferent look, the same he occasionally threw at her. At last he answered defiantly, 'One hundred.'

Chaudry watched him suspiciously. Finally, he snapped, 'That's one hundred too few!'

Malika breathed again.

The radio sputtered an indecipherable tune. Between disciplining Momin and the wood, Chaudry rapped his fingers absently. Faika sat beside him on a clay pot, stamping its voluptuous bowl with her unusually large feet, watching his craft closely. Her eyes shone with love for his alchemist's fingers.

'You should have been a boy,' Chaudry tenderly tugged her toes. 'You would have borne our tradition with pride.'

Momin responded by examining the ceiling.

'Don't provoke him,' Malika muttered, poking at the quilt, wishing there were a way to sew the warning into Momin's flesh, like a charm. But if her magic consumed Mrs Masood, it had no effect on her own family.

Just as she feared, Chaudry's pride was freshly affronted. He coughed spasmodically, as if his body needed to expel the insult, staring wildly at Momin who purposefully ignored him, then coughed more when he failed to break his son's recalcitrance. If Momin continued thus, Malika knew it was only a matter of time before Chaudry's rage turned into madness, just as it had with Shauqat and Moeez, and she would have to call the neighbours.

The situation was unexpectedly saved by Faika. At that moment, she dipped her palm into the lips of the clay pot, drew cool water and dropped them like pearls into her father's frothing mouth.

Clever girl, Malika smiled hopefully, feeling an interest in her daughter for the first time in the toddler's life. For though she was not even two, Malika was sure—so sure she would gamble anything on it—that the child had read the situation entirely: her darling brother would soon fall victim to her beloved father and only she could salvage them both. Her plan worked. Chaudry was so moved by the gesture he smothered her in kisses and dabbed the watery poultice over her cotton-soft lips. She spat and gurgled with glee, 'More! More!'

They had a mock water fight. Malika thought, without bitterness, that had she or, worse, Momin wasted their rationed supply Chaudry would have been livid. Instead he lavished it on Faika, while she circled around her brother to include him in the game. Though he remained apart, Momin humoured her with a smile, and when father and daughter settled down again, father and son prudently avoided each other's eyes.

Malika finished repairing the quilt, thinking how later this afternoon, while she worked at Mrs Masood's, she would not have to worry about her family. In fact, she could even leave

126

early for the pharmacy to restock Momin's medication. Content, she rose to announce lunch.

After the meal, on her way out, she paused in the doorway. Faika was exploring her tender armpits with rugged toes to better understand how both types of skin could belong on one body. She paused in mid-scratch and flashed Malika a gummy grin, as if to reassure her that she would remain perched on the clay pot-post and continue to play referee. The radio hissed, and Malika had a vision that Faika had prevented Chaudry from splitting Momin's head with it.

Chapter Seventeen

Early in December, M. Chauclet presented the Masoods a Côte Rotie. 'It's grown from the syrah vine, on the west bank of the Rhone. The name comes from your corner of the world, Shiraz, in Persia, the first home of wine.' He paused, as though his words were wine itself.

Mr Masood nodded drunkenly. His wife's cancroid fingers raced alongside her dupatta. She covered her mouth with it to conceal the mischief brewing there. Since M. Chauclet's arrival she had been in a quandary. Her dupatta was a garish green that smacked all the grace out of her pink, embroidered shalwar-kurta, and left her feeling like she had been thrust on stage without lines. A spurt of nervous giggles emanated, which increased her self-consciousness and excitement. She had never been centre-stage before.

M. Chauclet resumed, 'I could think of no more suitable way to commemorate this holy month, during which our children will join hands not only in a union of matrimony, but also of culture and commerce, than by drinking this.' He placed the bottle in Mr Masood's hands. While the latter opened it, the Frenchman continued, 'There are two varieties of the wine. I myself prefer the *brune*. Brunettes have so much more body than blondes.' He laughed heartily, looking, thought Mrs Masood, at herself.

M. Didier accepted the glass Mr Masood handed him and examined it in the light. 'I would trade mine for a blonde in a heartbeat.'

Mrs Masood sat at the edge of her seat. She wracked her brain for something to say to the audience who had come to applaud her act. She began to sweat. Her tongue grew.

Outside the Snow Angel seemed to wait for her as well. But the foul-smelling churail Soomla had taken Mrs Masood's speech away. It was really her grandmother's fault. She had purposely left the story of her great-grandfather and the churail unfinished so her own story enmeshed in it. 'Men are weak when they aim below their means, women when they aim above.' She understood it was all a conniving riddle. For she had followed in her great-grandfather's footsteps, and if he had walked backwards, it meant she had taken the lead, which is exactly what her grandmother warned she should not do!

While sifting her confusion, she heard M. Chauclet say, 'My wife—may she rest in peace—was from the region herself, and particularly fond of the Chateaux d'Yquem.'

He then proceeded to swallow his eyes, only they were, in fact, fern seeds. He produced more, and handed them out. One by one all three men disappeared. She alone remained on stage with her sole audience, the forlorn figure of her cabled mother outside.

'Where have you been all my life?' Mrs Masood asked her.

The woman smiled carefully, as though nursing a toothache, 'The same place you won't be when your daughter needs you.'

Mrs Masood frowned, for her mother too spoke in desert riddles. Then she thought of darling Laila, with satin cheeks and curvaceous lips, who must never know she had stolen her dowry.

The dear child, on discovering her designer necklace gone, had been so brave. She supposed the sweeperess must have taken it and banished her from the house at once. She had shed only a few tears, and fewer still when Mrs Masood showed her the ruby necklace with two fewer garlands than promised, and threw only a minor fit when the diamond set was visibly dim. 'The jeweller has cheated us!' she had shrieked. Then Mrs Masood assured her all salesmen were the same.

But Laila had not yet seen her wedding gharara. Mrs Masood planned on keeping it from her till the very end. The outfit—white as her in-laws—had to be made of a coarser material than promised, with fewer sequences and with embroidery not of genuine filigree but thread dyed gold. Mrs Masood hoped that if Laila saw it an hour before appearing before the groom, she would not have the time or presence of mind to protest.

'Who knows,' her boxwood mother muttered through aching teeth, 'whether that hour will ever arrive.'

Mrs Masood's despair grew. She remembered the terrible mess with Mr Afraz, the topiary specialist. He insisted his part of the deal had been kept; it was up to her to pay. When Mrs Masood refused, she only infuriated the wretched Soomla, from whom nothing could be hidden. The witch had gored her with fiery eyes and demanded the men be paid immediately, before she doubled their fee!

So her paradise lay strewn with boxwood needles, torn roots, vacant trenches and a cabled mother. How could she possibly wed her daughter there?

Her mother shrugged.

'I'm not asking you!' Mrs Masood shouted aloud. The invisible men fluttered, adjusting their positions to study her outcry. 'I'm sorry,' she apologized to the air. There was another flutter: they relaxed and continued drinking.

She heard M. Didier's voice extol the carpets her husband produced. 'You're lucky to have at your disposal the supple fingers of minors who can weave as many as three hundred knots per square centimetre. Adults can't even do a hundred!'

Which adults? Mrs Masood feared he meant her. Fingers darted all over the place, making her jumpy. Her fingers. She could never tie even fifty knots!

Slowly, M. Didier slipped back into view. He said, 'Only yesterday I read an intriguing article.' He reached for a newspaper clipping in his leather wallet and read: '"The Pakistan government has opposed western—and westernized eastern—propaganda against alleged child labour in Pakistan. The Minister of State for Labour and Manpower said that this propaganda was part of a well-organized conspiracy to reduce Pakistan's exports. But the government has successfully countered it and the sales continue unabated."'

Didier swung his long legs amusedly and read on, '"Eight thousand inspections were made..."' He looked up. 'They actually claim to have counted them!'

The effects of the fern seeds must be wearing off, thought Mrs Masood. All the men were visible again, though they careened a bit.

Mr Masood grinned, refilling M. Didier's glass. The latter continued, '"Eight hundred and thirty arrests were made for violations of the law."' M. Chauclet joined in the laughter. '"And a human rights ministry has been formed to take care of the issue *in a systematic way*."'

The room erupted. Mrs Masood bowed. Encore! Encore! M. Chauclet clapped, while Mr Masood was laughing so hard he began to cough. Mrs Masood bowed again. At last, she thought, applause!

M. Didier read and guffawed, guffawed and read: '"Pakistan has even signed a memorandum of understanding (MoU) to free its children of this dastardly curse."' Then he stood up, 'A memorandum of understanding? A toast!' He held up the glass of Chateaux d'Yquem and saluted the others. 'To the MoU: More of Us!' Glasses clinked.

Mrs Masood sat back sweating. She glowed. It had been a fine debut.

'Ah, business, business!' piped the Director of the French Cabinet of Exterior Commerce. 'How it weaves,' he paused so others could catch the pun, 'into our most leisurely moments. But enough! Today the wedding celebrations have begun!' Then he proceeded to explain in rapturous detail how the d'Yquem, of which less than two fingers remained, was distinctive. 'The sweet taste of the wine comes from the muscadelle grape, and the greyish mould that it attracts. The fungus sucks water from the grape, leaving it with an unusually high quantity of sugar and glycerin. We have lovingly named the mould *pourriture noble*, noble rot.'

Mrs Masood imagined herself to be the fattened, sweetened, dehydrated grape, and Soomla the grey mould covering her like a sickness. She scratched her skin and saw with horror that a fungus coated her fingers. It was spreading. She gagged, for it had reached her tongue. Without caring who saw, she groped for wine. The invisible Mr Masood returned to the hulk-like, hairy man she had known him to be. He warned she would be punished.

'Now,' her mother whispered, 'like me you too will be exiled.'

Mrs Masood finished her glass of wine. She had killed the mould. But now her husband would kill her! Terrified, she walked toward the wall-to-wall print of Versailles, hoping it would give as it had the night of the foot-massage. She pushed the sun-bleached lawns and radiating walkways, but the print was impenetrable as a wall. The plush burgundy carpet melted under her feet, and she with it. She was falling, just as her grandmother had warned.

And then she saw that the statuettes of the desert nomads, the ones her husband had given, had altered. It was a while before she identified the disparity: they had turned around. They no longer faced the edge of the desert, where sweet well water beckoned. They were headed for lusher grounds, a smug, city-smart gleam in their eyes. In place of the snake the man carried a Cote blonde, instead of the baby the woman had a dog on a leash. As she registered these changes, the smooth gloss of their sheesham skin metamorphosed into a suit on the man, and on the woman, into the finely embroidered dupatta that should have been hers.

Mrs Masood recoiled at the chintzy green cloth around her own shoulders. It was the same bold shade her Cholistani aunts would deck themselves in. Looking once more at the statuettes she sighed: they had escaped. The desert remained only in her.

'In us,' her mother corrected.

But then a gust of wind blew apart the last remnants of her shrubby flesh. The noose around her neck slid through the cables and landed on grass, soft as underwear. She slipped out of the shackles and wandered freely, invisible, like a spirit.

Chapter Eighteen

'But there's already a pit dug for the pond,' Momin told the handsome gardener. He wore a new olive-green sweater, and Malika smiled at how well it suited him.

The Pathan leaned on a spade in his characteristically thoughtful stance, shirtless despite the chill. 'Where?'

Malika shifted her gaze from the man's metallic poise to Mr Saeed's three acres. 'I don't see it.'

'Right there,' Momin pointed to a grassy section of the grounds, no different from any other but for a row of steps meandering toward it.

The Pathan marched jauntily to the spot. 'Here?' When Momin nodded, he smiled, 'Your eyes are sharper than mine.'

'That cover is phony,' Momin answered, pleased with his use of one of Saima's favourite words.

Peering closely, Malika deciphered an area shaped somewhat like an eight where the grass was a darker shade of green.

'It's turf,' the Pathan scooped out a lump. Inside was a hollow pool.

'How did you know?' Malika marvelled.

'She told me,' Momin shrugged.

'She? Saima?'

He shook his head, indicating the balcony ablaze with sun. 'She. Mrs Saeed.'

'Mrs Saeed?' Malika repeated. 'Or do you mean Mr Saeed. The Crow? Does he speak to you?'

Momin frowned, petulance clouding his brow. 'It's *Mrs* Saeed, up in the attic, who is the Crow.'

'But Mrs Saeed is dead!' Malika objected, wondering not only why Momin should think of her, but how he could know she had lived on the third floor.

Ignoring her, Momin cordially addressed the Pathan, 'Mrs Saeed likes the roses and wants me to thank you for sending the cuttings. She's also happy we're going to refill the pond. Though she won't be able to rest inside it she's glad other creatures will.'

The gardener, who knew nothing of either Mr or Mrs Saeed, patted Momin on the head. 'Of course. I'm happy to help such a fine boy like you.'

Momin beamed effusively. The Pathan swiftly tore off the turf till the entire pond was exposed. It was indeed shaped like an eight, or a woman's body.

'It's immense!' said the gardener, walking around the pool's outline.

'The stairs used to lead to a bridge, right there,' Momin pointed to the body's waist.

Malika stood speechless. She pressed her hands to her heart to calm it, while her mind reeled with explanations: could

Momin really have seen Mrs Saeed's ghost? Or had the widower begun communicating with him? Perhaps the child had found old pictures of the garden? Yes, this must be the case. And it must certainly have been Saima's doing. The girl daily fired his imagination just to alienate him from her.

For the second time since she had withdrawn him from the factory, Malika wondered if Chaudry had been right, if indeed the safest place for Momin was at the loom. Perhaps the child was too young to be free. How quickly he was changing and in a way she had not foreseen. What a vocabulary he had acquired! And what nerve! What would happen, five weeks from now, when he entered school? He might slip entirely through her fingers, just like a minnow.

She listened to the Pathan matter-of-factly list the pool's condition to Momin. The concrete was still strong and underneath, the copper pipe was still intact. In fact, once he had located the pump, all they would need was a new screen and a few rocks, and soon he would have a healthy pond with a dulcet waterfall attracting scores of dragonflies, other insects and naturally, birds.

Malika sighed. She had made Momin a promise and she resolved to keep it. She could never, despite her fears, have him pinioned again.

'It's big enough for fish as well,' the Pathan was saying. 'And,' he grinned, his cheeks caving in, 'water lilies. Those queens of all flowers.'

Momin listened with tremendous sobriety, like a manager. 'I've never seen water lilies.'

'Then you will. But this isn't the right season. Gardening is a lesson in patience.' He folded his arms over his tawny chest and added blunderingly, 'Mrs Saeed'll love it all.'

Momin looked victoriously at Malika.

She had been eyeing the balcony, searching for a sign—a shape, shadow, even an outline—for suddenly it had seemed she was being watched by a presence more pressing than the retiring Mr Saeed's. Now she blinked dumbfounded for she saw Mrs Masood. Her cheeks were puffy, and when she opened her mouth to speak, a worm-like tongue studded with diamonds extended like a tentacle toward Malika, who unthinkingly clutched at the gardener for protection. He smiled curiously. Embarrassed, she released him. The vision disappeared.

But Momin, his white teeth glinting, laughed triumphantly in Malika's face. I told you, he seemed to gloat. She recognized nothing of the child she had birthed. It was as if the illusionary tentacle, like a pernicious force, a witch's wand perhaps, had altered him forever.

Chapter Nineteen

Her grandmother had warned it was inauspicious to wander during a lunar eclipse but she was restless. Bottle in hand, she tiptoed in the waning light of her paradise, the gimcrack dupatta still pinned to her shoulders. She could not remember since when. On the far wall, once covered in morning glory, billowed the dupatta's shadow, like the grandmother's hair when she rode on Sirkash.

They had mounted him together on the night of Hinna's wedding, an honour none of the other women had ever enjoyed. Perhaps the old woman treated her to it since she was being sold for a handsome profit.

They strode toward the moon, full that night. Her grandmother had planned it so. The bride listened to the oxymoron of Sirkash's footsteps as he padded through the desert with heavy lightness and hushed intensity. His metal anklets kept the beat. The odour of mustard seed circled her head the way, soon, her aunts would circle it with money to ward off evil. She sat in front of the old woman, sibyl of the desert, watching her hair cast shadows on the silvery sand below to illustrate her counsel:

'Before Sher Khan overthrew the Emperor Humayun, before he was even born, his mother had a dream: the moon was entering her womb. She woke her husband to tell him. He responded by giving her a sound thrashing. "But why?" the pregnant wife sulked.'

Her grandmother's acrid breath lingered in her ears, demanding an answer. Thump, jingle, thump, Sirkash loped onward to the pitted moon, natant in the velvet sky. How many nights had she gazed at the galaxy from her place on the aunt-ridden bed? Thump, thump, thump, she had heard lizards fall on her pillow, and soul-sucking snakes hiss in her ears as her grandmother did now, confounding her even on the night of her wedding with desert riddles.

'Why?' the ancient sage repeated.

'I don't know, dadi,' she answered limply.

'Oh child!' She licked her cracked lips with a forked tongue and continued, '"I hit you," Sher Khan's father explained to his mother, "so you won't go back to sleep tonight after such a righteous dream, or you might forget it in the morning."'

Then she smacked Hinna hard in the face. A line of blood fell onto the bride's chin from the cut of her circular nose ring, symbol of the propitious moon. 'I did this,' she continued in her story-telling voice, 'to prevent you from forgetting that this is the best day of your life. Your husband is rich. He is offering a priceless opportunity. In return you must always obey him. Remember that.'

Hinna had wiped off the blood with her mirrored dupatta,

gaudy green to represent fertility. She snuffled in pain, watching her grandmother's hair coil and uncoil to the wanton lilt of Sirkash's footsteps.

They soon approached the lighted cocottes of the wedding party.

The flames flickered in the darkness, hundreds of them it seemed, welcoming Hinna to a new life her husband had promised would be sweeter than wine. Someone played a flute. Music rode the wind like smoke. She heard a dhol, clapping, giggling, and then a crystalline voice piercing the night in a melody that could melt dunes into springs. The closer they drew to the song, the less unctuous seemed the odour of mustard seed in her brain, and the taste of her own blood grew curiously pleasant.

Now, as Mrs Masood paced feverishly over nettles and dew, she looked up at the pale sliver of the moon. While the earth's shadow gradually slid off its surface, she saw in the bottle in her hands fermenting rot. It was too late for her: she had disobeyed her husband. She had consumed what he had forbidden, and in so doing, dishonoured her grandmother as well.

She held the bottle to the moonlight, then smashed it on the grass. Clasping her stinging throat, she searched on bent knee amongst the dishevelled topiary—her grandmother, mother, aunts, Sirkash, and all the other boxwood figures who had left her—for broken glass. Finding the right piece, triangular like a flame, she ended once and for all the sickening sweetness of her tongue.

As blood gushed in her mouth she remembered how it had tasted all those years ago. Strangely pleasant. Then an inner darkness flooded her mind, and she knew she was falling into a hollow pool from where she only barely deciphered a shrinking moon. But the lickerish orb, fully unclothed now, chose not to enter her womb.

Chapter Twenty

It was a different bus Malika rode on a week later.

In her weeks working at the Masood Paradise, Malika had had minimal contact with Mr Masood, barely catching a glimpse of him on Fridays when he whisked in and out of the house. Mrs Masood had explained he maintained a very tight schedule, even on weekends, when he lunched at 'the club'. She then rambled about how good he was, not expecting her to share his frenzied social life. But then her mood would change. Groping for more wine, she would weep, wishing he included her more. Malika rarely listened to Mrs Masood's complaints.

But last week she had found the woman curled on the gold divan, supported by pillows, a bandage wound around her head like a scarf. A tall man in a grey suit was frowning down at her while periodically talking over his shoulder at Mr Masood who, as if unable to be near the patient, sat in the adjoining dining room. His bloodshot eyes had momentarily brightened when

Malika entered the room.

'I must speak with you,' he had risen urgently. 'But confidentially, let's arrange a day. Next Thursday?'

Malika had taken a moment to catch her breath and decide how to respond. During this time she observed the factory-owner closely for the first time in her life. Beneath the red eyes hung skin as cushiony as a giant mosquito bite. His skin was oily, his stomach bulged, and as he waited for her response, he seemed to tire of standing and sat down again. Malika was shocked to realize that her own husband, without Mr Masood's wealth or status, maintained himself with far more grace.

'What has happened?' she asked at last, looking now at the living room, where his bandaged wife sat in a daze.

'Sit,' Mr Masood indicated the floor. His manner fluctuated between desperation and domination. She declined the seat. He continued, looking at her with eyes that bulged disconcertingly, 'There's been a terrible accident. We must discuss this further, but not here. Can you come to my office?'

Malika hesitated. 'I work at another house on Thursdays. This is my only afternoon free during the week.'

'Surely your employer will understand?' His large, purplish mouth hung open.

Malika moved toward the living room, partly to get away from Mr Masood's distasteful company, but also to ascertain exactly what ailed Mrs Masood.

The tall doctor was taking notes in a book and mumbling to himself. Mrs Masood watched reproachfully, the bandage around her chin damp with spittle that drooled incessantly from her mouth. When she caught sight of Malika her eyes softened, and Malika was reminded of a moth she had once seen emerging fresh from its hard, wet case.

Mrs Masood made apish sounds and excitedly scribbled something on a pad on her lap. The spittle rolled faster; she sucked it back like a baby. Then she handed the paper to Malika with eyes so gooey they made Malika sick.

'I can't read,' she said to the doctor.

He took the paper from her hands, and with the same frowning expression read, '"You've come at last, my noble rot!"'

'What does it mean?' Malika asked, staring at the spidery script.

'I'm a doctor,' he threw his notes in a briefcase and slammed the clasps shut. 'Not a wizard.' Mrs Masood's message fluttered onto the plush rug.

The doctor spoke over his shoulder to Mr Masood, 'Keep her on these medicines for another five days and call me if there's no improvement.' He left through the French windows, stamping past his patient's paradise.

Mrs Masood patted the seat beside her for Malika to sit. Only a month ago, she too had expected her to crouch on the floor, as her husband did now. But this realization brought Malika no happiness. She had got as much as she could from this family. Now she wanted nothing more than to leave their wicked ways. When Mrs Masood took her hand she cringed, remembering her first time in this house, when the twins were expelled. She had sensed, even then, a danger within these walls. Yet for Momin's sake, she had had no choice but to keep coming back.

Now, at last, it was time to leave.

When she rose, the sick woman puckered a mouth coated in sticky white layers of spit, as if expecting Malika to kiss it. On her blue skin hung beads of sweat. With her free hand, she scribbled again in her pad and pointed to the dining room, indicating that Malika should ask Mr Masood to read it to her.

Malika unwillingly took the note to Mr Masood, avoiding the longing gaze of his wife.

'Never mind what it says,' Mr Masood tossed the sheet aside clumsily, 'You must meet me next Thursday at three.' He gave her directions to his office.

Malika listened rigidly. When he had finished, she merely answered, 'No.' How could she tell Chaudry to stand up to him if she could not?

He studied her with swollen, bloodshot eyes, tinged with a faint glimmer of amusement. Slowly, he lifted Mrs Masood's discarded message from off the floor and read, '"It's my dying wish that in the final days of my life you be with me, so I can rest assured that I've been forgiven."' He folded it neatly, a gesture that was incongruously effeminate for his ungainly hands. 'I think you owe me an explanation. My wife has, since regaining consciousness, written obsessively of you. At one time she wrote that, if she should die before seeing you again, I must make sure you release her soul of its curse.'

He leaned into the chair and teased his moustache. His hands did not tremble now. She wondered then if any of the factory children had ever seen him, and if so, if it were his hands Momin used to dream of nightly when he moaned. Or perhaps it was those eyebrows, looming like rain clouds.

He watched her closely. 'I'm giving you a chance to do as I say of your own accord. If not, then I'll be most unhappy.' He clicked his tongue disapprovingly, 'I believe *you* are accountable for my wife's terrible,' he repeated, '*terrible* state. You do understand the exact nature of her accident, don't you?'

Malika vaguely shook her head. She had been so revolted by his drooling, clinging wife, and so determined to be rid of her, that she had not even bothered to ask.

Mr Masood gladly supplied an answer: 'She's sliced off her tongue.'

Malika winced, involuntarily covering her own mouth. She remembered the figure beckoning toward her from the widower's balcony, the whip-like appendage, pierced and dazzling, that had transformed Momin. And she recalled how Mrs Masood had complained, since their very first meeting, of the nagging itch in her tongue, how she had yearned to be rid of the discomfort. Was she then accountable for Mrs Masood's disaster? No! Mr and Mrs Masood were guilty, not she. She had merely taken what was hers.

'I'm a powerful man, with a loyal army of associates who'll happily take care of you.' He studied her closely, 'And your family. How foolish you are for thinking you can take my car and driver in the afternoons without my knowledge! I allowed it to continue. Your audacity made me curious.' She was crying now. 'Thanks to you, it was easy for my driver to track your husband down. He makes tables? I believe I even visited him once. A fine, hard-working fellow,' he rapped the dining table thoughtfully. 'Brings dead weight to life. But old. His own life could just as easily be a felled tree's. Who would not believe it an "accident"?'

Faint with despair, she asked him to repeat the directions to his office.

The passengers of bus nine ogled at her while curling their moustaches, just as Mr Masood had twirled his. She pined for Momin, whose frail presence had dispersed their lust on their very first ride together to the widower's house. It was hard to believe that was only a month ago.

She thought as well of Chaudry. She was grateful that, at

147

this very moment, at least they were both safe. In only a month, Momin would finally start attending school. No matter what awaited her at Mr Masood's office, Momin would go to school. She gazed out of the murky windows, vaguely registering the rows of paan shops, and the young boys who waited on the cars in front of them. Mr Masood loomed over her. He could easily have said whatever he wanted at the house. Why was he toying with her, forcing her to make this ride? She bit her lip, repeating that she would make her son's dreams come true. She was a good mother.

She had left him behind with the Saeed children and the Pathan gardener, who had agreed to stay with them so she could keep her appointment. Fortunately, he had not needed an explanation. She had merely asked for the favour and he complied, his work at Masood Paradise having ended.

Thinking of the Pathan lightened her spirits. She visualized him from head to toe, dwelling especially on the copper tones of his sun-dappled eyes. They always beheld her with immense stability, speckled with a hint of mischief. She thought again of their first meeting. The impression he had made on her then—that he was an ageless, wizened sage and playboy in one—had been correct. He was too merry to be always wise, too respectful to only flirt. He was, as the cool yet blazing hues of his eyes revealed, a balanced man.

Then there was his torso. Thinking of the smooth glossy lines of his shirtless trunk suddenly brought to her mind the lingams she had seen preserved in the National Museum, all those years ago with Chaudry. She smiled sheepishly but could not help herself. She followed those lines to their natural conclusion, imagining how they tapered to his crotch, swept his flanks and carved his thighs, like a river defines stone.

The bus stopped, and an old man beside her, encouraged by the dreamy smile on her face, butted her breasts with his elbow. 'Getting off here?' he grinned.

Malika shifted closer to the windows. 'Unfortunately not,' she scowled.

The old man cackled softly.

It was a tremendous effort, imagining one so beautiful as the Pathan in such hideous surroundings. When next he returned to her, he was standing beside the fishpond with Momin: head cocked to the side, listening to the boy's every need. Then Momin walked over to Saima at the pond's edge, and she saw them as they had been when she left for the bus stop: legs dangling inside, whispering together, periodically staring up at her father's balcony.

The memory unsettled her. She could not help feeling something menacing brewing in the widower's ancient home. Something only *she* knew nothing about. But as the bus flew by an old residential part of town toward the industrial centre and her stop, she repeated for the umpteenth time: Momin was safe. For now, it was time to collect herself for the meeting.

Chapter Twenty-one

Malika's footsteps were heavy with foreboding. In the year that Momin had worked at the factory, she had never seen it, his work-hours having coincided with hers at the widower's. It was simply *wrong* that she had to go there now, when Momin was free. Yet what was the option? She repeated the directions mournfully to herself, but was so tormented by an influx of emotion—her fear of Mr Masood, anxiety about Chaudry, determination to enroll Momin in school, anger at the world for offering her no alternatives, and more, impossible to distinguish—that she was soon lost.

'Where's Masood Carpets?' Malika asked a stooping beggar.

When he looked up she was face to face with the kind twin Khalil, the one she had expelled from the Masood Paradise. He wore a greasy kurta, torn at the throat, so she could see the skeleton of his once broad and athletic chest. His eyes too, despite their glorious shape and colour, had grown tinny, vacant. He held a dried melon rind in filthy hands, determined to suck more juice from it. 'That big building at the end of the street,' he answered gruffly, and walked away.

Malika was glad he had not recognized her and turned brusquely. But she had barely taken a few steps when the same hand tugged on her dupatta. 'I only know because I work there,' he nodded. 'I used to work in his house. No more.'

She walked quickly, tears streaming down her face. It was an ill omen! The image of his filthy, distended fingers, like Momin's barely a month ago, would not leave her. In attempting to free Momin, she had only shackled another. She bumped into a grocery cart, barely hearing the shouts of the vendor whose cauliflower heads tumbled to the ground. She tripped over a baby lying naked in the dust, kicked the pi-dog who limped after her, and failed to dodge the motorcycle that tore the skin off her ankle as it pulled into an adjacent lane, hurling a cloud of dirt into her mouth.

From the outside, the building resembled a multistoried shopping complex: whitewashed walls, glass windows with rusting grills, cars stationed in front. Malika trod despondently down an unlit corridor to the side, and climbed a staircase with no handrails. She reached a terrace.

It was very quiet upstairs. From this height and angle, the carpet factory was nowhere in sight. Of this she was unspeakably grateful. The traffic of the streets below grew remote, the people small and insignificant. She spotted a figure in a tattered shalwar-kameez hobbling by, and her heart pounded for fear that it was the twin. But she had no way of recognizing the features. They could just as easily belong to any one of the ten million others swarming the city.

To the north rose cotton and tea mills. A dense smog covered the horizon, leaving the ocean, just minutes away, only visible to a familiar eye. She imagined the bustle of the harbour to the south, the battered fishing boats drift away. She felt connected to the fishermen. They never knew what awaited them.

She remembered walking down the wet, rocking platform of the harbour with Chaudry, years before Momin was born. They had watched couples sail into the moonlight to catch crabs. Loose strands of her long, richly scented hair blew into his face as he held her, and she suggested they too ride out into the sea that glittered with fluorescent fish and city lights. But he had refused, saying there was no point in taking a life, no matter how small, for recreation. So mysterious was his sense of justice that he could defend a shrimp and abandon their sons in one breath.

On the terrace, her fingers rested on the colonial columns between her body and free fall. She knew this would become one of those moments in her life that she would look back on. Though to someone else perhaps forgettable, to her the instant had already grown timeless, like a bubble that separates from its surroundings even as it drifts through them. The bubble encapsulated the dearth, stench and struggle of her life in Karachi, yet it also held the warmth of her past with Chaudry, the memory of her sons, and her plans for Momin. It was like a prayer, and she prayed, most of all, for dignity.

She turned into the breezeway. Following Mr Masood's directions, she entered the second glass door to the left and informed the secretary that she was here for her three o'clock meeting. The ends of the young woman's mouth creased with disgust but Malika did not flinch—she was unashamed of her old shawl and rubber slippers. The secretary pushed a button, 'Sir, the three o'clock. It's a masi.'

'Ask her to wait a moment.' Mr Masood's voice crackled like Chaudry's radio.

'Sit,' the secretary indicated the carpeted floor. Malika ignored her, choosing instead to study the exaggerated poses of peasants in the paintings on the wall.

The door opened and a very tall white man with wide shoulders strutted out with a briefcase. His hair was cropped above the tyres of an immense neck, and his eyes small and fierce. He turned toward Malika, and they stared at each other as if the other were an alien species. Mr Masood hung in the doorway, beckoning her inside. The man said something to Mr Masood in, she assumed, English, about, she was certain, herself. He nodded. They both laughed. The white man left, and Mr Masood ushered her into his office.

It was stuffy and dark inside. She frowned, feeling she had gone through these exact motions before. Thick curtains covered the windows and a single light hung from the ceiling on a table littered with files. Mr Masood settled in a swivel chair behind the desk and gestured to her to sit on the floor. Malika found herself searching for the bejewelled armadillo to focus on while they talked. And then she realized that the dark room was like the widower's study, only more hostile. And there were no rubies to distract her from the dim light casting eerie shadows on Mr Masood's oily face, stretching his cheeks and fattening his lips, so he looked like a cartoon from the *Loony Toons* that Momin so loved. She wondered how many more times she would have to confront wealthy men in their stuffy havens.

'The matter is simple,' he began, rocking in the seat. 'My wife—for reasons perhaps only you know about—has committed a foul injury upon herself.' He paused theatrically, a technique Malika well understood as manipulative, yet her imagination was fired beyond control. How long had it taken? She must have sliced it over and over again, millimetre by excruciating millimetre. Or had the stroke been short and sharp? What had she used? Where was the weapon? And the tongue?

Mr Masood continued, 'She cannot speak, cannot eat, and has become somewhat of a burden, sitting there on her divan, drooling, doodling silly messages to us all. The fact is, Soomla,' he paused. 'Or should I say *Malika*?' This pleased him immensely. He began twisting a pencil on his desk.

So he knew her secret. This was no surprise. If the driver had told him who her husband was, he would have told him her name. But she resented the familiarity. It felt like a jinx.

Suddenly he sprang forward and resumed in a loud voice, 'My wife's timing couldn't be worse.' He flung the pencil furiously on the desk. It bounced silently onto the carpet where she sat. She stared at the pumpkin-yellow lines running down the length of its purple body. The paint must have been iridescent for it shimmered in the dark. 'Two very important contracts are to be sealed this month.' He rose from the chair and began pacing excitedly.

Malika shifted. She felt terribly vulnerable crouching on the floor while he stood erect.

'The first is my daughter's wedding to the son of a most influential westerner, a man whose opinion is of utmost concern to France. Even the Prime Minister listens to him! You can't imagine how lucky we are to befriend him. Nor what plans are being made to celebrate the union in his own home, after the ceremonies here. We must see to it that his needs are met on our soil too.'

He switched on the air conditioner, despite it being winter, and stood with his back towards her. In the pale yellow light his shirt flared like a balloon as the air conditioner droned. When he turned, his hedge of hair had grown manifold. Banging the desk abruptly with his fist, he concluded, 'This is a union that is good for our country.' Then he sat in his seat and was silent.

Malika dared not look up. In a voice she hoped was steady, she asked, 'What does all this have to do with me?'

'The second contract,' he answered, 'is between myself and a close friend of the influential Frenchman's. I believe you saw him outside moments ago.' Malika clearly recalled the beady eyes of the bulky man. 'It's a business matter, the details of which you wouldn't understand.' Then he rose again, and this time his pacing brought Malika relief for it kept his eyes off of her. 'My daughter's future father-in-law must not discover my wife's condition. He would think her insane, and fear the illness was in our blood. Not only would the wedding be cancelled, but the business contract too, for we need his approval to carry it through.'

He mopped his brow and returned to the air conditioner. 'Even before her accident, she had begun wandering through the house like a ghost, unaware that I was awake and saw how crudely she would loll on the divan, sipping the wine forbidden to her! A sinful woman! But I let it slide, for her activities remained unknown to everyone but me.'

The air conditioner hummed. It was the only sound in the room. She wondered what time it was.

'Since her accident,' he continued. 'I've been making absurd excuses to keep the Frenchmen from visiting our house. But the wedding's barely two weeks away. What then?' He inhaled deeply. 'You're the answer.'

She frowned: me?

'*You* can keep my wife at bay. She says you're a witch. If this is so, cast your spells on her. Keep her from making the slightest public appearance. Make certain that during the ceremonies she remains unseen. Not a single doodle, not a whimper, not even a sigh must reach the guests. I'll think of an excuse to explain her absence, you simply have to ensure it.' He then collapsed in his seat, exhausted.

Malika protested, 'But I don't make spells. I'm not a witch!'

He sat motionless, as if asleep.

'What you're asking me to do is make your wife invisible! How? How can I prevent a mother from attending the wedding of her own daughter? Am I to lock her in a room?'

'Why not?' he opened his eyes. 'Haven't you done worse? Take her away if you must! My driver will help you! Why not smuggle her into your prosperous employer's old mansion? I'm sure she'll not be noticed.'

'Bah!' Malika scoffed.

This struck a nerve. 'Let me remind you,' Mr Masood leaned forward, fully awake, 'that I ask you to concede of your own choice. If I were you I would. Do it for your husband.'

Sweat covered her skin though she shivered inside. So she was to become the crazed Mrs Masood's caretaker. Her mind tossed around all manner of possibilities—like the absurdity of somehow smuggling the woman into the widower's haunted home—but always returned to the one that might prevent her from keeping her promise to Momin. Mr Masood had mentioned nothing about paying her. If she worked more hours for him, and fewer for the widower, how could she afford his schooling?

'Tomorrow is a Friday,' Mr Masood's voice echoed in the dark whirlpool of Malika's mind. 'Take the day off. I'll tell my wife to expect you at our house on Monday.' He smiled, and with cheeks distended like a grotesque cartoon's, added, 'She'll be delighted. You may leave.'

She rose soundlessly and sped past Mr Masood's upturned purple lips, the secretary's disdain, and the paintings of women with serene faces hunkered on charpois, smoking hukkahs. She hastened down the breezeway, pausing on the terrace for air, the way Mr Masood had halted at the air conditioner. She searched for the bubble that, barely an hour ago, had reminded her of all that fortified her life. But it had drifted on.

Chapter Twenty-two

Two tides towed Malika's spirit that night, as she sat beside Chaudry, watching him eat. One instant she was on the verge of confessing all, freeing her heavy shoulders of the burden they carried alone. The next she recoiled at his wasting frame, with shoulders so much weaker than her own. In the matchstick brittleness of his neck bulged an Adam's apple with dogged prominence, warning her of his pride: how dare she meddle in *his* business! How dare she corrupt *his* son! And could she blame him? He had been cheated by her even more than by Mrs Masood! Wasn't that the truth? To rectify Mrs Masood's error, first she had repeatedly lied to Chaudry, and now even endangered his life. Hadn't she committed an even worse crime that Mrs Masood? No, she hadn't! *Her* motives were clean. *She* loved Chaudry. *She* yearned for his strong, sure fingers to hold and love her as only they had. But then the opposing tide pulled her away again, and she was left despairing of those same fingers, for it was the beauty and the folly of what they produced that was their undoing.

The curtain between their chamber and the store swayed dreamily, revealing glimpses of the headboard that simultaneously wooed and repelled her. Its round, bold design swallowed her like a vortex. She shut her eyes and felt herself churning in the motion of Chaudry's timeless circles, till she became the russet rings he gashed with his love. She moaned softly.

'What strange sounds you make,' Chaudry scolded.

She met his eyes. It was only two months ago, though it seemed like years, when they had beheld her with a trusting, adoring light. Now he did not even care enough to notice her sorrow.

She braced herself. 'You've changed.' Her voice was lower than she meant it to be.

He silently pushed away the plate of food.

'You show no interest,' she paused, searching helplessly for words that would not make him think her a pouting child. But she found no other way to say this: 'You never call me your little bird any more.'

He shifted awkwardly. 'I felt you didn't want it.'

'What made you think that?' She drew closer.

'It's you who's changed,' he retreated from her embrace. 'It's you who no longer spend Fridays with me. Instead you run off to the rich widower's house for a raise so you can spoil my son and teach him to disrespect my calling.' His voice trembled. '*His* calling.'

Malika winced at the manifold errors of his accusations. 'You mistake me,' she defended herself. 'A mother's last wish is to lead her son away from his father. You're both of one blood and blood should never turn against itself.'

They fell into a gloomy silence, in which Malika questioned the truth of her own words. Chaudry was right: she had encouraged Momin to deceive him, and now the boy had no respect for his own father, nor even for his mother. She had planted the seed of Momin's rebellion. As punishment, she was losing both him and Chaudry.

Chaudry glared unforgivingly, unmoved by her defence.

Then Malika shook her head, thinking, I *can't* take all the blame. And she recalled that fateful afternoon when she had walked into Mrs Masood's life and been mistaken for a churail. Was it her fault that Mrs Masood's error fooled Malika into believing she had found the answer? It all came back to Mrs Masood.

'Perhaps you're right,' she reached for Chaudry's fingers and smiled tentatively. 'I haven't even thought to tell you how beautiful the bed is. It's as you knew it would be—a masterpiece!'

He was dubious of her changed demeanour. But his fingers grew limp, inviting hers to stroke them. 'In two weeks it'll be ready, as promised.' He lowered his head pensively, as though wondering whether to return to his former, guileless self.

As Malika observed him, the events of the next two weeks flashed clearly before her eyes: the wedding festivities would begin while Malika successfully kept a slobbering Mrs Masood from dampening them. The dumb woman would spend the rest of her life in a daze, and Mr Masood would have his contract with the beady-eyed white man, a contract she was certain involved carpets, each one of which destroyed children like her own.

She squeezed Chaudry's fingertips, delicate as leaves. A new worry irked her: now that Mrs Masood was sick, who would buy the wedding bed?

She was worse than Mrs Masood.

Examining his wasting frame with teary eyes, she vowed to make peace with him. Inching toward a hug, she whispered tenderly in his ear, 'Promise me something.'

He looked up questioningly.

'Before the bed is sold, let's lie in it together.'

His eyes glinted with childlike pleasure. 'You're a naughty little bird!'

Chapter Twenty-three

It was not because she needed to explain her absence from his house that on Sunday, Malika hovered nervously outside the widower's leather-cushioned study door. She was certain he would not even notice. It was because she had become like a patient with a raging appendix that threatened, at any moment, to burst. The only way to remove it and save herself was to talk.

She had decided not to confide in Chaudry. Like her, he was too passionate. It was Mr Saeed's capacity to live as an automaton that drew her to him. She wanted neither sympathy nor scorn, neither blame nor vindication. She wanted to confess everything, and numb her pain. Mr Saeed, with his austere silence, would be the ideal listener.

But if only they could meet somewhere else.

The choking darkness and rancid stench of his nest reminded her of the recent encounter with Mr Masood, and Malika's courage failed her. She could not bear the stuffed and glittering armadillo with its snout propped open for others to marvel at the punctured tongue.

Shuddering, Malika turned away from his door and mounted the staircase to the children's rooms. The climb only heightened her unease. The awry steps were like the teeth of a monster, waiting for her to slip inside, which in her current, nervous state of mind, would be all too easy! Yet despite her fears, her large though malleable feet manoeuvred the stairs, flipping right, then left, according to the turns, till she reached the first floor, and the end of her territory.

After pottering around for an hour, Malika, searching for further activity to calm her, advanced to the top storey, where the dead Mrs Saeed's set of rooms lay and to which she had been forbidden entry.

She reached what might once have been a reception room. Glancing furtively about, she was surprised to find all the doors leading out from it thrown wide open. She had expected them to be locked. It seemed strange that a man who had withdrawn from life after his wife's death would not bother to remove or at least conceal every trace of the cause of his grief. But the third floor was an astonishing reminder of all that had been *hers*, and therefore, *theirs*. Cramped on bookshelves were vases of all sizes, each surrounded by layers of dust, and what Malika supposed were once rose petals. Beneath the shelves were filthy floor cushions scattered with magazines of slender white women with broad smiles wearing sleeveless tunics with large, flowery designs over bellbottom pants. Stuck to the teeth of one model was a congealed brown substance that had fallen from a tipped-over bottle: Mrs Saeed's nail polish.

Malika trod through the rubble, mystified and dubious.

She heard a rustling, and spotted a pair of feelers. Slowly, a cockroach tipped into view. It was scandalous, thought Malika, this violation of the dead woman's property. There were lipsticks, earrings, handkerchiefs, even bras. Was Mrs Saeed so messy? Or perhaps Mr Saeed had been in the midst of organizing her possessions when something terrible had happened.

Like the appearance of her ghost?

Malika tiptoed through the open doors. In one room was a bed of bronze, its headboard tapering like an obelisk, with leather padding where the newlyweds may have rested their heads, after a night of fitful lovemaking. The bedspread was bunched in an ungainly ball at one end of the mattress. Nearby was a matching dressing table, with a similar bronze obelisk rising from the centre like a minaret. The shape and form of the bed-set was cold. The artist had not lost any weight on account of it. Nor had he lost the sale. Nor had a powerful businessman threatened his life.

Afraid of what she might see in the dressing table mirror—the ghost of Mrs Saeed, a drooling Mrs Masood, or some gruesome image of herself—Malika quickly left the room. Before descending to the first floor, she took a final look at the petal-strewn bookshelf, and wondered again at the widower's decision to leave scattered his wife's belongings, exactly as they might have been when she died. The most absurd thing of all was the absence, amongst all this clutter, or indeed anywhere in the house, of even a single photograph of Mrs Saeed herself.

She climbed down, passing Mr Saeed's rooms—the doors were all shut. Back on the first floor, as if to make up for the dishevelled condition upstairs, Malika began cleaning again. She dusted Saima's collection of Russian literature. She pulled a few books out, remarking merely that they were enormous, their print miniscule, and that one had a cover of only a human nose.

Saima would often tell Momin that 'in no time at all', she would read him these jewels. Malika carelessly put them back, muttering that the girl was an utter fool.

She peeped out of the window. Down in the garden, Momin counted his minnows. He counted them every hour, afraid they would fly away. As she watched, he turned and looked up at the balcony, at the phantom of the woman in whose rooms Malika had just been. He gesticulated wildly to *it*. Then, in the rose bed, he began burying pieces of coloured paper. He had told her of this ritual to the Crow and shown her the drawings. They were of a woman who had an uncanny resemblance to Saima. Though undeniably a child's, he had captured the exact tone of Saima's hair, and streaked it with grey. He gave her large, singed eyes too. In one drawing the eyes were enormous swirls behind spectacles, as though he had tried to depict how they changed when enraged. When Momin was done burying the pictures, he looked up at the balcony again.

She sighed. He was growing in his own way.

With feather duster in hand, she twisted and turned down the stairs to the sitting room outside Mr Saeed's study. She began dusting the wood panels, studying the widower's door, wondering whether to knock.

The clock struck one. It was time to bring the children home. Tomorrow she must be at the Masoods. Now she would never find the chance to spill her sorrow at the threshold of Mr Saeed's indifference.

Momin entered through the front door and stationed himself to receive Saima. Malika brushed his cheek with a kiss.

In the car she realized that the wrath of Saima, lately dormant, was stirring again. The girl shifted in her seat, nursing a mysterious wound, waiting for vengeance. The opportunity did not present itself on the way home. Nor, to Malika's relief, did she choose Momin. She launched blindly past him, straight for the leather door that had paralysed Malika all day. She threw it open and stood in the doorway, obscuring Malika's view. Fazeel sprang upstairs. Malika ushered Faisal and Momin into the kitchen.

They heard snippets as Saima screamed: 'I've had enough! . . . As if I care! . . . Make me!'

A deep voice muttered strained responses. Faisal began to cry. Saima sobbed, shouting something about Mr Brown calling her to his office. 'He *picks* on me. He always fails my essays. And I worked so hard on my last story!' Momin tiptoed to the empty kitchen doorway and when Saima's hysteria grew, he turned helplessly toward Malika. She left Faisal and comforted her own son. They both ignored Faisal's protests.

There was silence, and then a crash. A door slammed. Malika was certain Saima had entered the sacred gullies of her father's underground gallery. She imagined him daubed in perspiration, loosening a shirt collar, following his daughter plaintively through the maze of his life's collection, while she destroyed them all.

Faisal had soiled himself. He tugged first at Malika's dupatta, then Momin's sleeve. The latter remained inert, then suddenly flung him against a wall. Stunned, Faisal bumped into Saima, who was at that moment strutting into the kitchen. She held the bejewelled armadillo triumphantly in her hands, and placed it with exaggerated delight on a platter. It sat amongst their lunch, clumsy and immense.

'How is everyone?' She smiled brightly at the bewildered eyes around her.

Despite herself, Malika marvelled at the pristine condition

of the dead mammal. Its rubies were like a well of clear water reflecting a flaming sky, and the blindingly brilliant diamond seemed to radiate heat. The shell itself was immaculate. She imagined Mr Saeed polishing it religiously with a hanky that he moistened with his own saliva, and that he perhaps tucked deep into his shirt pocket. He was a very peculiar man, she thought, letting everything but this dead beast fade away.

What would he do now, without his one source of light? Huddle for reassurance amongst the remaining relics, like a fallen monarch pacing through the passages of a crumbling castle? Weep to his files? Or fight like a mythic hero to bring his treasure back?

Similar thoughts seemed to run through Saima's mind for she eyed the doorway, tapping a fork testily on the rubies, and said, 'Let's see if he'll come out now!' The rubies tinkled like icicles. When no one appeared she picked up a carving knife. A smile pasted her face.

'Wait!' Malika intervened. 'Don't destroy the poor dead thing!' Her inverted feet rapped to assist the idea taking root in her forever-active mind. She took a deep breath and said, 'I have a plan. If it's useful to you, will you return the favour?'

Saima held the knife to the dead creature's throat. 'Why not?' She looked bored.

'I have heard you mention often that your friends' fathers give your principal gifts. That's why they don't get in trouble. Well, you could offer him something, and say it's from your father.' They both looked down at the armadillo.

Thus began Malika's attempt to mollify her rival. She offered it aware that the treaty could not last. Saima was a fiery youth who at best could be temporarily soothed. She understood too that it was Saima's waywardness that drew Momin to her.

Like a hawk, the higher she soared, the greater was her allure. Now Momin regarded his mother attentively as she at last soared closer to Saima.

'Is that so?' The corners of the girl's mouth rose very slightly as she mused. 'Perhaps. Well, why not?'

'Yes,' Malika maintained an easy glide. 'Why not? He may even give you a second chance to write a story. In fact,' she paused, wondering if her next suggestion would offend the girl's pride. She took the risk. 'If you can use it, I've a *true* story to offer. I've been waiting for an opportunity to tell it. Perhaps your principal will enjoy it. Especially with the gift.'

Saima rose with the sparkling relic, this time holding it with extreme caution, and smiled beatifically. 'Mr Brown will adore this beast. I'll say Aba bought it especially for him, as it's reminiscent of Kipling's "The Beginning of the Armadillos", and Mr Brown loves Kipling! Why didn't I think of that!' She strode out of the kitchen with plans to present her prize to a relic of the empire that had inspired its creation, a century ago.

Chapter Twenty-four

Malika arrived at the Masood's early on Monday morning, as promised. In return for Malika's 'brainwave', Saima had agreed to look after Momin during her absence, and to defend her should Mr Saeed notice, though they were certain he would not. In this way Malika was guaranteed her salary. Though uncertain if it would be enough to keep Momin in school, she consoled herself that he had already been enrolled for the first term. At the end of it, she could start fretting about the next.

Upon entering the neighbourhood of named houses, Malika thought about how complicated her life grew daily, how she was forever having to manipulate, dodge and lie, and all this for simple, honest needs. All she wanted was to give her family the nobility that *was* theirs by birth, though only she seemed to know it. Instead, she was caught in an ever-increasing cycle of deceit. How could she escape?

As she entered the Masood Paradise, she wondered if

Momin missed her. She knew the answer. Momin had plenty to do without her.

She determined to pull herself together, again. Despite her fear for Chaudry, and despite her anxiety about losing Momin to Saima and her world of fiction, Malika told herself to at least take credit for Momin's happiness and health. She had liberated him from the factory, and in this she had accomplished her goal. If in the process she had imprisoned the twin Khalil, ruined Mrs Masood, befriended her rival Saima, and jeopardized Chaudry's life, she was learning the price of success.

While treading absently up the swerving driveway, dwelling on things larger than herself, she was suddenly, unexpectedly, in the presence of a glistening, bronze torso. It reminded her of how she had quite recently likened it to a lingam. She blushed.

'What brings you here this morning?' The Pathan swaggered toward her.

'I've been asked to spend more time here.' She met up with him. 'Because of the wedding.'

He leaned in his typical fashion on a spade, to better reach her eyes. 'You've heard?' His chin pointed to the living room.

Malika grew sombre. 'Yes.'

He nodded, and studied her with purpose, till she turned away embarrassed. 'I told you once this is no place for a decent woman like you. Yet you return. I'm only glad I'll be here too.' He smiled warmly, his face only inches from hers.

She breathed his scent of flowers and sweat. 'So am I,' she muttered hurriedly. Then she asked, 'And what brings you here? I thought your work was finished?'

Sensing her discomfort—or, she feared, desire—he raised a dismayed hand at the garden. 'Look around. We've had to take it all apart again.'

She looked, grateful for the distraction, yet was horrified to find that all that was left of the paradise were gaping remains. The Pathan and his co-workers were sweeping boxwood needles onto the driveway, as only a few weeks ago they had swept handfuls of robust wild flowers. A skein of twine lay alongside them. They struggled to dislodge the last shapeless topiary but this only resulted in more debris being strewn, some of which caught in their hair in a final attempt at ornamentation.

'But what now?' gasped Malika. 'The wedding's barely two weeks away.'

'Well,' the Pathan frowned. 'There's not much we can do except fill the trenches. Mr Masood says he'll hide the mess with carpets. He has plenty.'

Malika sniffed reproachfully.

'Why are you really here?' The Pathan gently inquired. 'Surely it's not the money. The widower would pay more.'

What if she were to tell him her exploits, from the sale of Chaudry's table, to her 'witchcraft', to the interview with Mr Masood . . . ? Fearing his judgement might not tip in her favour she answered succinctly, 'Mr Masood asked that I look after his wife so she won't disrupt the festivities. When I refused he threatened to hurt my husband.'

The Pathan nodded sympathetically. 'Does your husband know?'

She shook her head. 'He mustn't.'

He sized her once more. His eyes were blue with hints of topaz that dazzled like the sun in a clear sky. He lifted her chin close to his parted lips. The other gardeners snickered. Malika ached with shame and yearning. She gently pulled herself away. The Pathan too was flushed.

'In the spring, I'll be moving north,' he spoke quickly.

'You're welcome to join me.'

'But your wife?'

'She stays here with my family. I've been offered work in a place more beautiful than you could imagine, tucked in clouds, above all worry. Your son would love it.'

Malika retreated, this time with disdain. 'You would leave your wife, just like that? And then leave me when your work is finished to return to her?'

The Pathan shrugged. 'You don't want to be here.'

Malika's temples pounded with outrage. 'I could never abandon my husband!'

'Oh?' his sunny eyes twinkled. 'You wouldn't even consider it?'

He seemed to insinuate that she already had.

She stormed away, entering Mrs Masood's living room feverishly, only to be greeted by the spit-soaked, blood-blotched bandages strewn on the luscious Persian rug.

The patient writhed in narcoleptic sleep. Maika was reminded of the first time that she had seen her from these very same French windows, when she had not thought it possible to behold a more humiliating spectacle. Yet she saw it now. Mrs Masood's milky white cheeks were covered in a rash, her fine hair was oily, dusty and haphazardly pinned back so as not to interfere with the strips of cotton wound around her head, to keep her once bud-like mouth from biting on the stub of her freshly amputated tongue.

The prospect of spending the next few weeks with this nightmare loomed before Malika.

Mr Masood, refreshed by his morning shower and reeking of Ocean Blue, marched into view.

'Ah, you came!' He feigned surprise.

'As you wished,' she muttered.

'Very good,' he beamed. 'Well, keep her company.' He did not look at his wife. 'Cheer up. She'll be delighted to see you. You'll see.' He straightened his tie, snapped shut a briefcase, and was gone.

Malika paced restlessly through the house. She had never entered the bedrooms before, never had the interest. But anything was better than sitting with *her*.

Laila's bedroom door was ajar. She herself was nowhere. Malika sat on her bed and bounced lightly on its plush mattress. Her fingers dwelled on the lilac covers with scalloped trim. The curtains matched them, as did the cushions of a love seat near the foot of the bed. All the furniture was pristine white.

Malika wondered who was helping Laila with her dowry now. Or was it complete? She reflected detachedly on the final worth of the endowment, aware that it had been somewhat reduced by her demands on Mrs Masood. But in the grand scheme of things, she decided the decrease could not be significant for Laila, though it made such a difference to Momin. Even if Chaudry failed to sell Laila's wedding bed, even if Mr Masood bullied her, Momin would go to school.

The springs of the mattress creaked. There was nothing else to do but listen. Was this how the next two weeks would pass? She yawned and lay her head on one of the silky, heart-shaped pillows propped against the headboard. On the bedside table a large lilac clock ticked sonorously. She turned on her side, to face the window. The gardeners continued clearing the lawn. The Pathan stood apart from them, his bronze back to her. His muscles were tense. The further she sank into the soft, feathery depths of Laila's bed, the easier it became to admit that he had seen through her, and unlike her, had nothing to hide. He did as he pleased and was honest about it. In contrast, she thought only of her family, but lied. He was free. She had never known a woman like him.

She rubbed the pillow with her fingertips. Laila's bed was sweeter than the rope one Malika currently shared with Chaudry. But it was not as noble as the one he built. The two tides that simultaneously pushed her to and away from her husband troubled her again. For an instant, she imagined spending her life with Momin, far away from the Masoods, Saeeds, twins and all the tortured others whom she did not even know yet. She could be with the Pathan, when he wanted. She could pray for God to protect Chaudry from customers like Mr and Mrs Masood. She would no longer have to spend her days with a crazed woman, to protect him herself.

Tears like inkblots darkened the lilac covers as she accepted that her princely Pathan and his promise of a mountain berth, ensconced in clouds, high above the Masood Paradise, would remain a dream.

On the divan, Mrs Masood was slowly awakening from a codeine-induced sleep. The drug had not entirely left her. It dulled the ache in her mouth, kept the stump of her tongue—absurdly like a parrot's—still.

In the first few days after the cut, unable to accustom herself to the void, she had moved the remaining protrusion frantically, convinced that she was dreaming, and that in her dream she had accidentally swallowed her grandmother's fern seeds. This was what had made her tongue vanish, and soon it would reappear. She wrote to the doctor, explaining her optimism. But he had frowned and impatiently explained the wound was permanent, and that it would never heal unless she ceased playing with it. He gave her a plastic bottle of white pills. Fern seeds! When she refused, he injected them. While falling asleep, she had understood that now her tongue would never return, for the doctor was part of the conspiracy. Her suspicions were confirmed when, upon awakening, she had discovered her face was cabled like her topiary mother's. Then she believed that like her, she would soon escape. But she had told no one. They would punish her.

That was over a week ago. Lately she was either too doped to worry, or too worried to crave anything but dope.

She propped herself phlegmatically up on one elbow, and fumbled for the plastic bottle. She carefully loosened the bandages that fastened her chin. She raised a cup to her lips and threw back her head to swallow. The pill grazed the stump of the tongue, with which, despite the codeine, she tasted blood, which she believed to be wine. Then blissful analgesia set in.

From the French windows she observed how the winter sun blanched the once-yellow garden walls. Or were they purple? No, pink, like the ceiling above her, where a lizard the size of her arm now crawled. She shifted, afraid the reptile would fall on her mustard-scented pillow. Its tail was fat. It swayed.

A group of men worked in the garden, their bare feet smeared by dirt where there should have been emerald-green grass. Then there was emerald-green grass. She sighed, wanting nothing more than to stare and stare at her idyllic picture.

If only the lizard were not in it. The creature scampered till it was above her pillow again. She hunkered at the edge of the divan, squeezing her pillow. Its eyes were inky and sidling. They followed her without moving. They swayed.

Monitoring the lizard from the corner of her eye, she looked out again. One gardener in particular interested her. She liked how the drawstring of his shalwar gathered neatly at the waist so when he moved, the folds of his shalwar shimmied. When he crouched on his heels and drank from a water hose, she recognized thirst. When he licked his parched lips, she tried to mimic him. But, failing, she touched her lips with her fingers. They were puffy and numb. He turned his head toward the house, not at her but an adjoining room, which she remembered belonged to someone important in her life. But she remembered no names.

The gardener's eyes were intense. She had seen that expression somewhere before. His thick brows bridged above an aquiline nose because he frowned. He mouthed words to that important someone in the adjoining room. She gazed confusedly, wondering what was being said. Then her curiosity dissipated. The lizard scurried behind the portrait of the buxom virgin who gaped placidly like a cow.

Mrs Masood felt something tickle her back. The gardener's face drifted in the vast cavity of her mind and she played with it as she wished she could her tongue. It became a piece of a jigsaw puzzle that she tried to fit on various types of clothing in different landscapes. Three-piece suits in the living room. No. Sherwanis at receptions. No. Night suits, cotton pajamas, jeans, silken handkerchiefs, cufflinks. Still negative. Jinnah caps on Eid. Cold. Turbans. Warm. A bright orange scarf wound as headgear. Protection from the sun. She was very close.

The face belonged to a man hunched on a dari in the sand. He bargained fitfully with others, convincing them to purchase his cattle. She was a girl with nipples so young they burned against her glossy rayon kameez, orange, like the man's scarf. She knew she looked ludicrous. It was almost as if her grandmother wanted her to attract attention. She was leered at by Afghan mujahideen with bullets strapped to their chests.

She had been dressed up for the fair by her grandmother and aunts. She remembered this. It was the clearest recollection since the night of her mishap. They had allowed her to go to the fair as a rare treat, accompanied by a man who lived behind a drape, in a segment of a thatched-roof hut rife with lizards and ghosts.

Mrs Masood shifted again on the divan, nervously scanning the walls for the lizard.

The gardener was walking toward that someone in the next room. Mrs Masood leaned forward, watching him vanish from her line of vision. The man in the orange scarf was animated, for he had succeeded in selling the camel for a good price. The animal jerked onto its feet. The girl kept sitting, facing the thick black callosities on the joints of his legs. They were spongy and sagged, like the skin of a reptile.

Mrs Masood got up and peeped behind the portrait of the serene virgin. She took down the portrait. Shook it. Now where was the lizard?

She was awoken by the Pathan kneeling on the windowsill. He slid inside with ease, as though his muscles were made for this. She was winded with awe and longing.

Once inside, his bare soles sullied the deep, hyacinth carpet. 'I shouldn't be here.' He stood at the foot of the bed where she lay.

She sat up and studied the baneful footmarks. 'No, you shouldn't. For so many reasons.'

'My coming was involuntary. Like falling.' He smiled.

She looked over his shoulders, out of the window. 'Where are the others?'

'Lunch. It's noon, you know. You've been sleeping.'

So he had been watching her sleep. She was vexed, not so much by the audacity but the sneakiness. She had thought him brave. She said so.

'But I am honest,' he answered. 'Cowards don't admit their actions. Besides, I only spied for a minute. And now,' he looked around, as if for a prop, 'here I am.'

Malika realized it was the first time she had seen him without his spade. It was as if he missed a limb. He was nervous. This amused her. 'Don't wait for me to offer a seat. It's not my house.'

'Well,' he folded his arms, still looking for that prop. 'We can pretend it is.'

She laughed then, and he said it made her pretty, and given his recent defence of his presence, which she found ultimately irrefutable, she had to believe him. 'Then sit down.'

He sat on the love seat.

Malika feared the mark he would leave. She said, 'I'd make tea but the kitchen's past the living room and *she* might awaken.'

'Next time.' He smiled. His craggy figure would not fit into the folds of the settee. He perched on its edge, leaned back and leapt to the edge again, desperate for air.

Malika, though entertained, did not know what to say, and for once the gardener was tongue-tied too.

'Everything's so soft in here,' he said at last. 'And the smell, it's like soap.' He stood up again, and rested a leg on the foot of the bed and an arm on the knee. He was slowly falling into place. He looked at her intently.

In the hollow of her mind, she heard him ask, is the bed more comfortable? She had stopped breathing, she was sure of it, yet her heart raced. How could it when there was no oxygen to pump?

She tucked her hyperactive feet neatly beneath her hips, inadvertently offering him room.

It was not behind the portrait of the serene virgin.

She trod very nimbly with a fly swat over the pattern of paradise on the burgundy rug. The lizard hid in the sheep's wool. It was trying to outwit her. Its skin changed colour, according to the dye, though never to wine red. It was not *that* clever. It must be in the inner field, where there were long, blue tendrils it could blend with. It could do so because the blue dye came from a plant of the mustard family. She was proud of this bit of knowledge. She even knew the name of the plant: wod. No, that wasn't it. But it began with a *w*, and then an *o*. Woe? Wok? Woo?

She dusted the blue tendrils with the fly swat, then dragged the swat across the dense layer of loops like a lawn mower. She mowed the yellow, flowering shrubs—the plant this pigment came from was familiar to her too—brown, thistle-like leaves, orange fountain. Perhaps the beast lay *under* the carpet.

She threw away the fly swat and began to roll the rug. She intently examined every inch of the carpet's looped foundation like a scientist looking at a new specimen. At last she conceded: there was nothing new to discover here. She began to roll the pink wall-to-wall carpet underneath the rug. It was like moving the earth. She fought the adhesive that stretched like chewing gum and made a horrid sound, as though her insides were tearing. The adhesive caught in her fingers, or, she was caught in *its* fingers, and the fingers enclosed her like vines. But she would not give in. Not, of all things, to a lizard. She reached once more for the fly swat, and with it, scythed the creepers, leaving ugly blotches on an already blotchy floor.

Next, the furniture. The velvet couch was a rock. The

statuettes pebbles that were flung recklessly aside. The divan a felled tree that she dragged off, inch by inch. The liquor cabinet, once all the bottles were tossed, too was eventually removed. She rolled and rolled, till the carpet touched the sandalwood table. This was the mountain. She tried to lift it. Were it not for the bandages wound around her chin, the strain would have caused her to bite even the remaining stub off. She tried dragging the table like she had the divan, pushing it like the couch, smacking it like the statuettes. She torqued and twisted, heaved and hauled, but it was as stubborn as a camel.

He touched the hairless skin of her inner forearm. It bristled with joy. He untied her drawstring and touched her hairless inner thigh too. His sinews bulged like snakes, were harder than tree trunks, and Malika did not protest. It was too early for more guilt. No, too late.

'For once,' she whispered in his strangely delicate ear. 'I want to get what I want, straight.'

Breathing heavily, Mrs Masood collapsed on the cylinder of piled carpet. She remembered only that her fern seeds were lost. She began to keen.

Under the patch of carpet beneath the table the lizard skulked.

Malika moaned. She had dismissed the far-away crashing that intercepted the Pathan's loud breathing. But now she pried herself free from under his chest. 'What was that?'

He pulled her back. 'Me.'

'No, listen.'

She heard a puppy yelping, or a kettle whistling. She knew

from the way his kisses weakened that he had heard it too. The whistling rose to an owl's screech. She bolted out of his arms and flew down the corridor.

Upon seeing what awaited her, Malika crumbled beside Mrs Masood.

The living room was in utter disarray, worse even than the garden. It was as if a jewellery box had been shaken like a bag of bones, till every stone, metal and chain link had splintered, hammered and split. She would be blamed for this. Mr Masood had demanded that she watch his wife. And she had broken her promise. She had broken so many promises! 'Stop!' she shook the woman's shoulders. 'Stop!'

Mrs Masood did not hear or see. She swayed from side to side, wailing like a widow.

'What do you want?' Malika screamed. The howling only increased. Malika cursed. She cried. She was desperate. She held Mrs Masood's glue-swathed hands. 'Please tell me what you want!'

Mr Masood had left no emergency phone numbers. Of course not, he would not tolerate an emergency. That was why she was here.

Think. She wrung her sticky hands, and for a tenth of a second contemplated how impossible it was to wring sticky hands. Then she remembered the doctor. He had spoken to Mr Masood about some medicines. She must find the doctor. No, there was no time. She must find the medicines. She frantically began rummaging through broken bottles, torn canvases, shattered vases, shards of wood, clumps of wool, all of which stuck to her godforsaken icky fingers. She looked under the couch, and over and around the inverted cabinet—thinking, how could she have moved all this alone?—and hurriedly rolled open the pink carpet, then the burgundy one, and there, in the centre field, lay a plastic bottle. She hastily loosened Mrs Masood's spittle-soaked bandages. But the patient refused to open her mouth. A livid Malika hurled the bottle against a wall.

'I don't think she'll notice me,' the Pathan whispered, poking his head around the doorway of the corridor.

'Do something,' Malika's feet writhed.

He nervously tiptoed into view. Mrs Masood still keened. He tried to pry open her jaws. But she was strong, strong enough to single-handedly demolish the living room. He was forced to smack her unconscious. Malika, incapable of seeing the lacerated mouth, turned her face away. The Pathan forced two delicate pills down Mrs Masood's throat.

They worked till five o'clock, rearranging furniture, mopping floors and brushing the carpets. They beat the pink one, then stamped on it, venting their frustration while simultaneously glueing it back quite nicely. But the liquor bottles, vases, ashtrays and everything that could possibly be broken, were lost forever. They said nothing to each other.

Just before five, when he would have to leave Malika to confront Mr Masood alone, the Pathan sat her down. Though he held her close, she would not stop shivering. They stared at Mrs Masood sleeping soundly on the divan. A lizard, barely thumb-size, popped out of her kurta collar and scuttled confusedly away.

Chapter Twenty-five

It was Mrs Masood's last day in paradise, though she did not know it. Neither did Malika, who arrived in the morning just as Mrs Masood was stuffing fern seeds down her throat. The medicine was beginning to have its multifold effect when the mute noticed her maid, or ayah, as she referred to her fondly in the notes she never read.

Upon seeing Mrs Masood awake Malika groaned.

Mr Masood's cologne wafted into the room. He walked briskly past the living room, then left for work without breathing a word. Malika knew his silence was meant to intimidate her, but she was grateful for it. The only thing that repulsed her more than his wife's company was his. However, she was counting her blessings too soon, for he quickly returned.

'Watch her,' he ordered sternly from the front door.

'I will,' she answered, without looking up.

He waited in the doorway.

Mrs Masood squiggled frantically on the loose squares of paper she always kept beside her. Malika impatiently returned the notes. 'I've told you before. I can't read.' But she continued writing.

Mr Masood drummed the door with his stubby fingers. 'See to it you do,' he repeated. 'See to it all. See to it all, all the time.' And he continued drumming.

Malika loathed him. 'I can only do what I can.'

'Sadly,' he waved his arms around the stripped environs. 'That's not enough.'

'I told you yesterday, I'm sorry. I was cleaning your house, doing my servant's duty. Your wife was sound asleep. How was I to know what would possess her when she awoke?'

'You must never leave her side.' He ceased drumming, and shouted instead. 'Never. How many times must I repeat my orders?'

Mrs Masood was very excited. Pages upon pages tumbled onto the rug.

They had been through it all yesterday evening. Mr Masood had thrown at her a string of curses, and Malika had bowed her head in silence to acknowledge the mistake, without Mr Masood guessing *which* mistake she regretted most. She swore to never let it happen again. He had all but slapped her. She had sworn again. He had accused her of deliberately planning the disaster, called her the devil's angel, a witch. She had sensed that beneath his fury, he was afraid of her. She had cried inside, for alas, he was granting her the kind of power she did not seek.

When a man like Mr Masood feels threatened, she thought now, it is enough to drive him insane. He charges like an enraged bull, again and again. There would be no peace without either one's defeat. This was what Chaudry had tried to warn her of, when they argued that chilly night in early November, when the lumber for Laila's wedding bed had just arrived.

But Malika was still unable to surrender. Last evening, she had bowed her head in silence, but she would not do so again. Knowing it was foolish to answer back, she nevertheless could not restrain herself: 'You're exciting your wife. The doctor's orders are to keep her calm.'

He slammed the door. It rang with her error. 'I've been thinking.' He put his briefcase down very slowly, and sat on the couch. Malika was struck by the contrast. He was big but soft, and the slightest exertion made him gasp for air. His wife was small and dainty, but in her madness had a physical force believed to exist only in her husband's sex. It suddenly struck Malika that she had as much reason to fear Mrs Masood's virile strength as Mr Masood's feminine wiles.

'I've been thinking a lot,' he panted. 'And I've reached a fair decision.'

Mrs Masood was watching him and drawing his features. Malika was surprised to find a distinct likeness, even though his shaggy head was greatly exaggerated: it hung past his shoulders and became a braided tie. Mrs Masood reached for a small box of crayons and chose silver.

'I've decided,' continued Mr Masood, 'that you're to take my wife away. I had suggested this on Thursday, when we met at my office, but then, trusting in your sense of responsibility, decided against it. Obviously, I was wrong: you aren't to be depended on in *my* house. So you'll take her to your widower's mansion, and after the wedding, bring her back. Safe. If she, I, Laila or anyone else in whose interest I serve is hurt in any way by your sly charms and curses, beware. I know a witchcraft called friends in right places. Or,' he paused, brushing an imaginary speck of dust off the gold-painted buckles of his briefcase. 'If you prefer, your husband's dead if you resist me ever again.' He opened his mouth wide and laughed. Malika had never heard or seen such a laugh. It made Shauqat or Jamil seem sweeter than doves. Mr Masood's eyes filled with happy tears. His wife drew a face that was all mouth. 'Ah,' he sniffed and sighed, attempting to pull himself together. 'Your husband is a poor old haggard dear. I hope you love him.'

He rose then, and stood in the doorway like before. 'The car will be back for you within the hour. I expect her gone when I return. In a few weeks, I expect her to return without a scratch.' He smiled, and at last he left.

Mrs Masood nodded off to sleep. The drawings of her husband lay on the rug. In one his head was a mass of cobras.

Malika leaned back into her seat and waited for Mr Masood to send back the car. She had no choice but to take Mrs Masood to the widower's, and sneak her into one of his forbidden rooms. And what if he came to know? Surely he would not remain indifferent to his household any more?

There was no use in speculating. In attempting to clear her mind of the burden Mr Masood had placed upon it, she thought of the one for which she had no one to blame but herself. I'm an adulteress, she muttered. The words impaled her. Her crime was still too fresh to reflect on with anything but naked horror.

Mrs Masood snored in her bandages. The immobilized lips, struggling to break free, twitched and flapped, taking on a mysterious life of their own, like linen pegged on a line. Mr Masood had made Malika the clothespin. If she snapped, Chaudry would die.

Chaudry! If he learned of her betrayal, this would kill him too. Ah but she loved him! How tenderly he had rubbed her loins with mustard oil when she was young . . . The thought was abandoned in mid-current, like a castaway, for it was too painful to think of him beyond a staunch resolve to keep her promise to Mr Masood.

She gazed with despair and longing out at the garden, as Mrs Masood had done for most of her married life. The Pathan was there, prudently avoiding looking in. His movements were less controlled. He did not lean on his spade with the taut snaky arms that had held and anchored her yesterday. He paced restlessly, often hovering around the other gardeners to make himself known as their boss. Conscious that he invaded their space, the others glared challengingly at him. Once an argument erupted. Malika never supposed the Pathan capable of such a temper. She heard nothing, for the windows were shut, but saw the once-sunny eyes now flicker with a different fire as he gesticulated wildly. She felt sad for them both. What if the opponent was Chaudry? She imagined a confrontation between lover and husband, and realized she would defend the spouse. But what absurd loyalty was this!

I'm an adulteress, she repeated, still unable to grasp the immensity of the charge.

Her attention switched back to Mrs Masood's lips, wavering like a blind sea anemone feeling for food.

She sighed, preferring instead to observe her disgruntled lover, who must surely be wondering at the outcome of her meeting with Mr Masood. He would never know. They must never meet again.

Malika burst into hysterical laughter. There were no limits, absolutely none, to the mess she was in! She laughed uncontrollably, imagining what the ashen widower would do if he came across a woman asleep in his dead wife's obelisk bed, a woman who, believing herself haunted by his housekeeper, had sliced off her own tongue! She laughed unstoppably, imagining Saima mock Mrs Masood's insatiable lips sputtering like a horse's. She was oblivious of awakening Mrs Masood until the latter blinked, innocent as a newborn. Malika pressed the stitches in her sides.

Fresh from her nap, Mrs Masood's mind was open as a cavity waiting for gold. She recognized the ayah, though she had quite forgotten her name. Her round face with the bent nose and wide-set eyes were quite sweet, especially when her long, green locks tumbled onto her shoulders. The hair seemed to screen her eyes from the sun, like a camel's eyelashes. She leaned forward to see if her lashes were as long as a camel's. But the ayah retreated with fright. Mrs Masood attempted a pout but her bandages were too tightly bound.

The silly, slurpy gesture made Malika woozy. She said, 'Why don't you go back to sleep?'

Mrs Masood shook her head like a child being forced to sleep.

'All right,' Malika frowned. 'Don't.'

A grateful Mrs Masood leaned forward again to take her hand, but the latter pulled away. She kept pulling away. Mrs Masood tilted her head sideways and studied her: this was no ordinary ayah. She quickly scribbled a note, then offered the conversation piece, wanting badly that it be taken.

Malika perceived the yearning in her eyes and thought, God has a wicked sense of humour. Now that this greedy, fraudulent woman was finally learning to love, she was an embarrassment. Malika pocketed the note. Mrs Masood tried to smile with gratitude. Malika's stomach curdled.

She looked outside again, wondering how her lover was

coping now. But where was he? Malika sat up. The Pathan had disappeared. Her heart ached. She had wanted the option to sit and stare at him one last time. But this too had been denied her! And then she allowed herself to remember what she had been trying to forget: how yesterday afternoon he had unbuttoned the top two buttons of her kurta, and strung her breasts with kisses. The recollection made her limbs weak and head light. Her blood rushed to the centre of her body, the crotch, making it heavy as a magnet. No! she tried to dismiss the yearning, and thought of Chaudry. 'A poor, old, haggard dear. I hope you love him.' That she, a woman who had spent all her life thinking of her family, should so betray them! What had she done! What was she doing now, imagining her lover's naked limbs parting her own!

Mrs Masood was folding squares and began arranging them one by one on Malika's lap.

Malika jumped, upsetting the offering. 'What on earth are you doing?' she screamed.

Mrs Masood recoiled guiltily, extending a timid finger to the rug, where, among the drawings of Mr Masood, lay the animal figures, trees, flowers, birds, and her favourite, a boat with paper fringes rising from its centre like a fountain. She wanted the ayah to admire how well she had duplicated the carpet's imagery. Instead, the ayah was angry.

Malika slouched heavily back into her seat. 'Don't touch me,' she hissed.

Mrs Masood tried to pout again, then returned quietly to her drawings. She glued, pasted, and clipped diligently, laying her labour gingerly on the rug for the ayah to approve of when her anger subsided.

Malika wiped her sweaty forehead. She glanced listlessly at the drawings. They were no better, but no worse, than the ones

Momin offered ritually to the ghost of Mrs Saeed's rose bushes. She felt feverish. She could not believe how completely the wily Mrs Masood had changed.

She heard a car's engine, then saw the copper-hued Honda Saloon halt outside the front door. It was time to go. How should she explain to Mrs Masood? What lie should she concoct now?

Malika twirled the animal figurines in her fingers and in a sudden gesture of magnanimity said, 'My son would love these. Why don't you give them to him?'

Mrs Masood nodded eagerly.

In the driveway, Malika guided her cautiously into the car. She looked around for the driver. He was standing by the gate, talking to the Pathan. Malika quickly turned away from them. What were the two discussing? Her heart raced. Perhaps he was asking where she was headed, thus trying to guess the outcome of her meeting with Mr Masood.

Well, no wonder she had not spotted him from the living room! He was busy inquiring obliquely after her!

The driver now hurried to the car and got into his seat. Malika climbed in with Mrs Masood. As the car reversed past the gate and onto the street, Malika exercised immense strength and looked away from her lover, though acutely aware of his perturbed eyes drifting from one passenger to the next.

It was Mrs Masood's first time outdoors since her injury. She squinted at the sun, wishing her grandmother had not dressed her in such ludicrously chintzy clothes, for she was attracting so much attention. She squeezed the ayah for protection. A tall, handsome man watched her. She had seen him somewhere before.

Chapter Twenty-six

Though the ancient doorkeeper was always a little bothered, nothing alarmed him. When Malika rapped on the gate with a bandaged woman trembling in her arms like a rabbit, he mumbled irritably but let them in. Then he fumbled with his heavy key ring and opened the door, all without asking a single question.

It was almost twelve o'clock. The children had not yet returned from school. Malika ushered Mrs Masood into the kitchen. She could not wait to gaze upon her son from the windows as she used to. He was reclining on his side on the banks of the pool. He wore grey pants, a white shirt and a grey sweater: Saima's school uniform. It was much too big for him. Though his hunched back was to her, she could tell how animated he was, for his free arm waved excitedly, and the sleeve of the over-sized sweater made rings in the air. His tiny feet tapped together in the spotless tennis shoes she had bought for him from the first installment of her salary from Mrs Masood.

'That's my son,' said Malika. 'You could say you gave him those shoes.' She sniffed accusingly.

Mrs Masood was growing uncommonly attached to the ayah. She clung to her arm and watched closely, lest she leave.

'In fact,' said Malika, trying to shake her off, 'it's in return for those shoes that your husband now asks me to abandon the child,' she paused. 'For you.' She jerked her arm frantically, 'I'll have to leave him, you know. I'll have to leave him here while I work for you . . . ' She twisted abruptly but Mrs Masood was like a jellyfish. Pushing could not help. She began peeling the tentacular fingers off her skin but as soon as one loosened, the others fastened more tightly. 'How would you feel if you were forever separated from your child, no matter how hard you tried to be near him?' She was shouting now. Beneath Mrs Masood's fingers, her flesh turned red and itchy. She scratched furiously, first her own sores, then Mrs Masood's, while the latter's eyes popped with pain. 'Get off me!' Malika's screams quickly turned to tears. 'You're a demon! A witch!' It was as if the past two months' hurt, hope and despair all pressed upon her with each pinch of the mad woman's skin, and she felt her world shrink, as though she were drowning or lost in the gullies of an old walled city. The more she panicked, the tighter grew the fingers. Her only option was to yield.

'You win,' she gasped. 'You and your wretched husband.'

Mrs Masood's sea-anemone lips wavered in a smile, for there was something in the ayah's demeanour that assured her now. The round-faced peasant had ceased looking out of the windows and focused entirely on her. With her fingers Mrs Masood drew the words 'thank you' on Malika's arm, causing them to erupt in goosebumps.

Malika steered her out of the kitchen and up the slender spiral staircase. She was keenly aware that there was not enough room for them both. But Mrs Masood insisted on walking shoulder to shoulder. The two women rubbed like Siamese twins lodged together at the hip. Malika tried not to panic. They slowly made it to the first-floor landing.

Malika paused, and stretched. 'These are the children's rooms,' she indicated two closed doors.

Inside the door on the left, one woman imagined a dense, dark carpet strewn with fanciful tales that crept inside her son's young mind like a disease, while the other imagined she could hear her grandmother snoring. In the door on the right, one saw toy soldiers leaping on Land Rovers, while the other saw a camel's long neck wind around the curve of a child's neck like a sah pina snake.

Constricted again, they climbed to the second floor. Again Malika paused, though this time very briefly. She shrugged to loosen her shoulders but with such agitation that they knotted further. She whispered, 'These are Mr Saeed's. You are never to enter.' They mounted a final time, till the staircase opened onto the centre of the reception room laden with glossy magazines and the sound of tiny bodies scampering.

Mrs Masood listened attentively, wondering, whose feet are those? She quickly examined the ceiling. Instead of the white stucco ceiling crisscrossed with cobwebs, above her was a low thatched roof rife with beady-eyed reptiles. They could fall, thump, thump, thump, smack on her mustard hair. She had been brought back to the desert. This was no ayah. She turned her eyes on Malika, making them beady.

Malika did not notice. She was pointing out the different rooms. 'These are the dead Mrs Saeed's. Upstairs is a terrace, also not available to you.' She contemplated taking Mrs Masood to the room with the obelisk bed, and this made her smile, not without some bitterness. But thinking better of it, she whisked her ward into the smallest, sparest room of all, around a corner not immediately visible from the staircase, reached by climbing three sidling steps. 'This will be yours.'

It had a roof of glass, a section of the terrace floor. There was a small rectangular window at the top of one wall, too high to reach. A bedroll lay piled on the floor. A toilet and sink stood at arm's reach from it. This had been the chamber of the dead wife's ayah, stationed close enough for her to have heeded Mrs Saeed's every need, yet far enough to keep her apart when unwanted.

Mrs Masood had told Malika enough for her to know of the woman's spare, isolated, Cholistani past. It was ironic then that she be lodged in this room, and still further ironic that she do so under circumstances that had rendered her even more unwanted than the ayah in whose room they stood. Malika was surprised to feel some pity for her. She too had suffered: she had been poor. This was a fact Malika had never been able to accept before, not till this very moment, when Mrs Masood was poor again. The admission made her, in Malika's eyes, not only more pitiable but also more culpable, for her powerlessness was Malika's burden.

Mrs Masood resembled an animal newly released from a cage, so the scale of the room perfectly suited her. Anything larger and she would have recoiled. After much cajoling, she moved forward, prudently sniffing the air before each step. Eventually she released Malika's arm and began marking her new territory. She strode from one windowless wall to the next, claiming the blankness. Then she looked up at the square of clouds floating by.

Still moved, Malika explained, 'Your husband wants you here till the wedding festivities are safely and successfully over. I'm confident the owner of this mansion won't object, as long as you leave him alone.'

Mrs Masood was not listening. She had discovered a previously unknown phenomenon. Every twelfth of a second, a dazzling radiance appeared in the turquoise expanse above, and every thirteenth, a rain cloud obstructed it. Also astonishing was that there were no lizards.

Malika quietly locked the door behind her. As she descended the staircase in her customarily tense, focused manner, she worried about the new arrangement. Though it was unlikely that he would, what if Mr Saeed noticed Mrs Masood and objected? How could she possibly explain? What with his allowing Momin to stay with her, her secret absence from a job he still paid her for, and now this clandestine sheltering of a mad woman under his roof, she had taken so much more from him than she had a right to.

In less than half an hour the children would be home. In the kitchen, she hurriedly prepared them a surprise lunch: daal soup and omelettes spiced with hot green peppers. Momin had disappeared from the pond's edge. She knew he was stationed at the front door.

Soon she heard the heavy metal gates creak apart and an engine rattle. Saima entered the kitchen, holding Momin's hand. Upon seeing Malika, her eyes brightened. 'I didn't expect to see you again so soon!' She squeezed Malika's hands with affection. 'I wanted to thank you. Your plan worked! Mr Brown keeps the armadillo on a pedestal, the highest point in his office. He has entirely stopped picking on me and has even suggested I write another story, which he'll be happy to mark again!' She beamed at Malika with her luscious, almond eyes.

'You're welcome, of course,' Malika answered dismissively, though not unkindly. At the back of her mind she was aware that in one day she had elicited a sickly sweet amount of gratitude from two previous opponents.

Momin looked at her with an altogether new expression. He was like a well-groomed student, reserved and well meaning, who has been taught to say a polite, indiscriminate hello. Malika clutched his free hand, a gesture she knew was too rough for one as refined as him. 'I so miss being here with you,' she could not restrain herself. 'Don't you?'

'I'm okay.' He pulled his arm away like she had so recently pulled her own from Mrs Masood. She released him.

Sensing his response had somehow not been enough, Momin looked at Saima then added, 'Saima says I've gained weight.' When this too appeared inadequate, he tried, 'So does the Crow.' Then he gave up.

Faisal was crying at Malika's knee. She sat him icily at the table. 'The food will get cold.'

'I'm starving,' squealed Saima. 'Thanks for preparing lunch! I've so hated having to do the housework! Are you here to stay? Say you are!' Malika nodded. Saima continued bubbling, 'Remember mentioning you had a story to offer? Well, I've been thinking. Since your first idea worked so well, maybe you can once more bring manna to my life.'

Malika fed them in silence, stealing glances at her son while Saima chattered. He had grown. She had committed adultery. She could never look at him with a clean conscience again.

She would confess everything to Saima, saying it was someone else's true story, and Saima would transcribe it in letters Malika could never read. She would tell her how this someone had failed as a mother.

Yet Momin would still go to school. She had made this possible. And because of it, some day, he would forgive her. Maybe when he had a degree, and a fine job.

After lunch, they mounted the stairs to the children's room. Malika suddenly remembered Mrs Masood's notes to her, tied in a corner of her dupatta. 'Perhaps these will inspire you,' she said to Saima, untying the bundle.

'Love letters?' Saima gawked. 'You have an admirer, eh?'

Malika smiled. For an instant, the memory of the Pathan revived her and she wanted nothing more than to bask in the memory. But she tossed it aside, determined to forget him. 'No,' she answered. 'They're notes from a woman who, if the messages intrigue you at all, can be met easily enough. Her role's important in the story I have to tell.'

'What fun!' Saima already had her nose in the scraps of paper. 'They're quite mysterious. I shall enjoy decoding them.' She looked at Malika flirtatiously and patted the space beside her and Momin, 'Come sit with us.' Malika sat stiffly down. That Saima should *allow* her to sit with her son! The girl distributed half the scraps to Momin, whose lips promptly began moving to decipher the scrawl.

'They haven't been numbered,' Saima continued unfolding. 'It's hard to follow her train of thought. But really, this makes the unravelling all the more challenging.' She looked at Malika, anticipating excitement in her too, but she sat silently. 'Oh, don't be so glum!' When she still got no response, she continued her running commentary, perhaps a tad less jauntily.

'"You've come at last, my noble rot,"' read Momin aloud, proud of his developing reading skills, looking up at Malika.

Chapter Twenty-seven

Momin was delighted with Mrs Masood's paper figurines. Every morning that week, he scrambled fearlessly up the coiling staircase, while Malika followed slowly, nervously balancing a tray of Cerelac with hot milk and soft-boiled eggs for Mrs Masood's breakfast.

It was the eve of Christmas Eve and Malika was terribly nauseated. Soon she would have to witness Mrs Masood unwind her bandages and chew her baby food with a tongueless mouth that she moved slowly like a camel. Malika could not bear the intense concentration in her eyes, nor how her hands rose and fell to aid the delicate process. She wanted to throw up each time Mrs Masood winced when a morsel grazed the stump of her mangled tongue. Most of all, Malika's nausea was caused by watching Momin remain calm through it all.

On the morning after Mrs Masood's arrival, Momin had quietly followed Malika to her room. He had not been surprised to see her at all. In fact, he had told his mother he was glad the Crow had finally decided to let him near her, and happier still that Malika also befriended her. 'See,' he had smiled. 'I told you she lives up here.'

Malika, surrendering, had muttered, 'Hmm.' His world was beyond her grasp. Mrs Masood had become the Crow, when earlier it was the dead Mrs Saeed. Even more perplexing was his adoration of the wife of the man who once enslaved him.

Nothing about Mrs Masood repulsed him. He found her altogether normal, albeit a good deal more interesting than his mother. Before Saima returned from school, he divided his time between the budding garden and the wilting industrialist's wife. They exchanged gifts. She gave him an endless stream of notes that he saved for Saima to unscramble, and paper animals, whose quality was greatly improved by the crayons and markers Momin provided, courtesy Saima. In return, Momin gave her an hourly update of his garden, with scintillating details of the silvery minnows, gargoyle-like orange carp, and their more shady cousins, the little black carp. And while Mrs Masood held him, he demonstrated how a slimy toad leaps from a human grasp.

Mrs Masood was equally delighted with him. Ever since the day her ayah had taken her to the desert, she had been good only for bringing food. It was Momin who satisfied her need for companionship. For the first time in her life she was in the presence of someone who did not judge her, and hence was unlikely to persecute.

Mrs Masood swallowed her pills, rinsed her mouth with Listerine, tied fresh bandages and settled back into the thin eiderdown that was her home. Malika gathered the old strips, in some patches stiff with spit, in others soggy, to dispose of later.

'Hold still,' said Momin to Mrs Masood as he sat on the cold floor, his back to the wall, drawing her. With charcoal, he made her bandages into the ashen mask of a crow, her perpetually waving lips the black wings, and her legs a ruffled tail. This pleased him immensely. Malika tried to smile.

Mrs Masood could not understand. Perhaps the boy was showing her a black cloud. When I was bathed by gilded feet, she wrote, I was hot. She yearned for a breath of fresh air on her clammy, calcified flesh. Through the glass above, she saw the wind tease a puff of white cloud, and prod sluggish grey ones smoothly along. Twelve and thirteen, she wrote, and passed the scrap to Momin.

He raised his crooked, charcoal-stained fingers thoughtfully to the bud of his mouth. He must understand what she meant. He was a studious child who could not easily quit.

Mrs Masood counted the clouds, struck once again by the mathematical exactness of her discovery. Right on time, she scrawled.

His fingers fell from his lips, leaving behind black prints. 'I just don't know,' he sighed. 'I'm as blind as a mole.' He had used the simile correctly, and this made him smile. 'I'll keep trying,' he assured Malika, who needed an altogether different assurance.

Mrs Masood was charmed by the hairy smudge on Momin's upper lip. Her eyelids were growing heavy with sleep, and as they fluttered, she imagined the moustache blowing high into the opalescent sky, like a feather spinning upward, defying gravity.

Momin chatted happily about an underground telescope-like device that Saima had given him. With it, he was able to peer into the tunnels the moles burrowed. He described, in impressive detail, how the subterranean creatures scurried both forwards and backwards like fish, with powerful front feet that jutted right out of their shoulders, their eyes and ears completely obstructed by fur. 'They use feelers always covered in dirt,' he explained, 'that look like a thick moustache with food in it.'

Mrs Masood heard the word 'moustache,' and, comforted by the knowledge that Momin understood her, fell into a deep sleep.

'Saima says there are no moles in Pakistan, only shrews,' he continued. 'But for once I think she's wrong.' He somberly added, 'They have twenty-two feelers.'

When Mrs Masood snored, the mansion seemed to rise and fall, and a sigh emanated from its empty rooms. Mother and son listened silently together. Their separate worlds quaked, gliding further and further apart.

These days Saima was at her dynamic best. Mr Brown had made her class prefect and she was the object of her classmates' envy. She knew she must continue pleasing the principal, and pursued this goal with head held high and a confident smile, doling out goodness to everyone. Securer now, she gave Momin a more constant, less hungry love.

When Malika sat beside her that afternoon, she tapped the point of her pencil on a blue notebook and mused, 'You've worked for us so long and yet we're only just becoming friends.'

Malika glowered, though she did in fact look forward to the afternoons when Saima wrote her story. She thought about them in the mornings while waiting on Mrs Masood. Not only did they help lighten her load, but it was flattering to be the object of someone's attention. Even Saima would do.

In between hearing and recording Malika's tale, Saima trotted up to Mrs Masood's room to clarify things for herself.

She accepted the stranger's presence matter-of-factly, the way she never could her father's absence. Momin accompanied her. Malika did not think it necessary to join them.

Occasionally, she begged Malika to twist her feet backwards. Whereas this had once revolted her, now, coupled with her newfound awe of Malika's insights and the dignified, mysterious reserve with which she carried herself, she felt sure the feet-turning might well be an indication of something supernatural. This made her shudder with a horror that kept her interested in the story, and certain that Mr Brown would prize it above all others.

Momin, however, was not interested. He left for the garden to paw the earth around his roses. An hour later, he burst excitedly into the room carrying a cardboard box with a ribbon around it, asking Malika for the keys to the Crow's room. He had exhumed all the drawings he had been burying over the course of the month as a ritual to her roses. Now he wanted to present his work to her. He untied the bow and showed his alarmed mother an array of the most meticulous sketches she had ever seen the child produce: delicate tendrils of earth-toned hair blowing across an aquiline nose and heavily painted eyes drawn in pen-and-ink that really did resemble the once beautiful Mrs Masood.

Perhaps the finesse of her son's lines would one day equal Chaudry's. Like his father, what he lost in physical stature, he made up with a vision that frightened her, for where did it lead? The boy was slipping out of her hands. She gave him the keys.

Chapter Twenty-eight

Momin sped eagerly upstairs, the box of portraits in one hand, keys in the other. He would tell Saima later how his heart raced, for it was the first time his mother allowed him up alone. He entered softly as a ghost, and stood panting before the sleeping woman. He lay his offering beside her pillow. Her bedroll was torn. He felt how the cold from the bare floor must steal into her bones. Her lids fluttered with agitation. He had seen his father visited by sleep but it was not like this. The Crow did not rest.

A circle of sunlight filtered through the glass above. He stood in it, watching his spotless tennis shoes sparkle like the surface of a pool. He wished he could somehow drape the sun across her face.

Overhead, clouds drifted silently along. Though delighted to have the Crow so near him, he thought it cruel to confine her. Perhaps she was happier when able to lurk freely through the house as a spirit, or blow with the clouds like other crows.

The circle of sunlight vanished. Momin knelt on the chilly floor and gently touched the fluttering eyelashes. They were as fragile as a butterfly's wings. He waited till a single lash fell onto the tip of his crooked index finger, thinking how, unlike his mother who made him ashamed, the Crow had never drawn attention to his deformity. But Malika felt his scabs each time they were together, even in front of all the big men on the minibus. And worse, she covered them with henna. He looked like a girl, or even more insulting, a bride! When he married, *his* bride would never wear henna!

Momin sat a while, enjoying these last few minutes with the Crow. It was expected that *her* fingers be dry and horny. Perhaps, when she woke up and flew away, he could watch her from this very spot, in the square of sky above. It would be her way of staying close to him. He would draw her hovering in the glass.

Then he tiptoed out, leaving the door unlocked.

Chapter Twenty-nine

The carpenter Chaudry waited for her in his store. It was a little after midnight. She had put the children to bed and was rinsing the dinner dishes outside. The water was frosty, the night cold and crisp. She sneezed. A moon danced in the aluminum bowls. She shone it in the direction of the store, on Chaudry's impish face poking impatiently out of the curtain. He was tickled by her coquetry. It made him want her more. The water hardened to ice while she rinsed, tinkling against the aluminum surfaces like Saima's fork tapping the rubies of the armadillo.

At last she turned off the tap and slid into his arms. It was their first caress since her adultery. She avoided his clear, adoring eyes.

Stark naked, he carried her to the wedding bed, completed only an hour ago. 'I'm too old for this,' he giggled between fits of coughing.

But for an oil lamp, it was pitch dark in the store. A draught seeped underneath the front door and the curtain flapped. The oil lamp spun very slightly, revealing the pattern of the headboard in spurts of soft light. Malika fingered the design as Chaudry arranged the bedding and began to undress her. While he gingerly pecked her erect nipples, and his gentle, sturdy hands traced the contours of her stomach, she moaned with pleasure though her eyes grew teary with guilt and defeat. She thought, this is how he shapes wood.

Mrs Masood was awoken by a full, unveiled moon and the circle of gold that ringed it. Looming directly above her glass roof, it draped the room in a blue light that was her closest encounter with anything holy. She was at ease. She did not immediately reach for her pills. The light glowed on her flesh as though someone held her. She counted twelve, then thirteen, and scribbled, No obstacles tonight, thank heaven. Then she looked back up at paradise and sighed.

The light also cradled a shape beside her pillow that at first she mistook for the pillow itself. But when she tried laying her head there it caved in, and she was sorry to have crushed a bow.

He was bony, his penis cold, breath acidic. But his delicate arms were warm somehow, warmer than *his*, warm enough to help her thaw from the frost of the diamond-cold night that advanced ominously to Christmas Eve morning. Turning her face away from his, she inhaled the thick perfume of the cedar, rolled on the virgin bed, and raised her hips so he could reach the bend of her thigh and squeeze her rump.

His beard brushed her navel. She was damper than a cedar forest. Her fingers spread over the headboard, clasping curling vines, tongues of grass, petaloid palms that fit into hers and yielded scented water that she drank, imagining his back were as strong and unblemished as the carving. She remembered Momin's drawings, how closely they had begun to resemble his father's, and for an instant, ceased moaning in compliance. But then he opened her thighs and she remembered the Pathan's torso. She smelt his odour and wondered if he smelt her too.

It was the colour of a bruise, Mrs Masood decided, looking at the red bow in the blue moonlight. It suddenly occurred to her to look inside the box. This thought gave her pause.

Then her skin burned as though someone had slapped it. Perhaps her grandmother. The blue light was her grandmother.

Like a child stunned by a foreign mark on her skin, Mrs Masood studied her bruised arm. Would it bleed?

She could open the box.

Chaudry whispered, 'Are you proud of me, little bird?'

She wound a leg across his shoulders, and tickled his ear with her foot. He groaned with desire. The foot began to turn backwards. She released the headboard and touched his sunken cheeks, kissing him full on the mouth. She thought, today the wedding festivities commence. Laila will marry without her mother. Beginning to shiver again, she pulled Chaudry closer. She thought, I should not think of this now. I should not think of this at all. But Mrs Masood haunted her most private hour like a stubborn itch, and she tensed. Poor Mrs Masood: her only child wed without her! When his time came, she could not imagine herself absent at Momin's wedding. She was sorry for the woman in the ayah's room, and sorrier still that her anger toward the thief was beginning to thaw. Why should she forgive her! Why should she when her husband tormented Malika by threatening Chaudry's life! Why should she!

She was crying. Chaudry licked her tears away, whispering, 'How tender you are.'

She smiled at his innocence. He believed she cried for the beauty of the bed! Perhaps, in a sense, he was right. She did cry for him, for his art, for the Pathan, Mrs Masood, and of course, for Momin's future. He would go to school, but ... ah, here was the question she dared not ask: would he stay? Or would he, like his father, prefer to use his hands ...

Her eyes fell again on the headboard, at the light waving across it from the oil lamp, and she swore the vines undulated like locks of hair, now concealing, now revealing, images of the child's portraits. With what patience and love his crooked fingers could capture Mrs Masood's once picture-perfect features! He had a gift, of a kind she did not possess. It allowed him to see the pond before the Pathan unearthed it; to talk to the stern Mr Saeed while tending his dead wife's roses; to love filthy, ugly moles and a tongueless, mad woman; to persevere in reading and writing; and to devote himself to an upper-crust maiden who was less dependable than a loose wire in a thunderstorm. Thus far, he was a survivor. But could he endure the pressures of a low-income school?

Ah, the Saeed mansion both liberated and spoiled him. It had given him milk, meat and flowers, but it also fed ambition of a type Malika had not foreseen. Saima confused the child with tales of her own education. In less than a month, he would discover that the system available to him not only contained no 'fun activities' like art, story-telling, cricket, field trips or May Queen Balls, but no fans, desks, and often, not even a room. His teachers would not have read the books he expected to be taught. They would find his curiosity a threat, and it was no secret that a hot, ill-paid, ill-respected teacher, when provoked, used the stick. If Momin wanted to climb the ladder of scholarship, he would have to be submissive.

But after Saima's world, Malika feared a public school would be as crippling to Momin as the factory. Then what if, like Chaudry, he decided skill *was* indeed higher than education?

Miles of shimmering sand stretched between her and the bow-bound cardboard box, which she now identified as the well of sweet water. Thirsty, she rose and walked around it. She circled and circled, once, twice, twelve times. On the thirteenth round, a jagged line of clouds crossed the face of the full moon. She was reminded of another face, the face of a sweet child, a maiden who was to become a woman that very day, she was sure of it, hadn't she herself on the night of a full moon? The face rotated like a wheel, or clock, and she thought to consult the face of her wristwatch: 1:05.

The girl-child wore a lilac dress. Lilac, the colour of the bow. If she opened the box it would reveal more about the moonchild who stirred in her very womb.

She thought, no one will buy the bed. His pain tomorrow, and the next day, and forever, will be impossible to live with.

'I've made a bed fit only for princesses like you,' Chaudry pushed his middle finger inside her. 'My forefathers would be proud.'

Well, she thought, tightening around the digit, once the wedding is over, and Mrs Masood returns home safely, perhaps we can begin again. Mr Masood will leave me alone, Momin will go to school, and Chaudry will sell the bed to a new customer who will pay fairly.

She clenched, pulling his finger up, and up, turning onto her side, enveloping his stick-like legs with hers. His nose was in her scented hair. She tried not to scream.

'You'll wake up Faika,' he whispered, not without joy. He slid a second finger in.

'Yes,' she breathed.

He kissed her hard to dull the screams.

She rolled onto his pelvis and he entered.

She thought, *my* forefathers would be ashamed.

There she was, a creature resembling herself, but younger, heavenly, virgin, serene. Mrs Masood felt herself unworthy of the likeness. Her fingers traced the comeliness of the face in the box, with skin smoother and whiter than cream. She sifted through the numerous drawings, moved to tears by the gift, on this full moon, of the immortal duplication of her own dear child. She clasped the neatly cut squares to her bosom and her mind swam with thoughts that ceased eliciting a pattern even to herself. She knew there was something more to remember, to understand. It involved the moonchild, the dull orange hue appearing in place of the night sky, the round bold lines of the hand that drew. Something important was to happen today.

She arranged the squares on her bedroll like pieces of a puzzle: here was a naked curve of a shoulder, here a sheet of chestnut hair curling up at the ends, and here thick spectacles framing the dark eyes that only added to her confusion. There was a perfectly aquiline nose with a large, circular nose-ring that hung above full, oval-shaped lips that breathed not a word.

A colourless light settled on a corner of her bed. The blue light had vanished. It had been hours since she last had her pills but she did not want them. She wanted to know what she knew

She stared with foreboding at the rising sun.

'You are unsettled,' he said. 'Is it her? You'll see, the madam has changed. Don't you remember with what courage and humility she returned to pay more for the table? And all on her own! She'll pay the honest amount for my honest labour, and you'll see I was right to continue serving the fair woman.' He continued chirping optimistically, now looking at the wedding bed, 'Have you ever seen a cleaner finish? Superior joints?' Then he embarked on a detailed explanation of the beauty of the dovetail joint, which few carpenters attempted today. 'If you look carefully, you'll notice how it creates hidden joints . . . '

Malika imagined the mute in her room above Mr Saeed's. Nothing would be further from her mind than the bed, or even the wedding. At this very hour, she was probably sleeping, dreaming of her desert past, and imagining her grandmother beside her. In a few hours, she would undoubtedly attempt to communicate her fears with Momin. But the poor child was so far from knowing the mad woman's truth. Just like his father.

She pried herself loose. Everything reminded her of the wasted labour. What a life was his! God give him strength, she prayed. Protect him from the evil of despair whenever it descends.

'I'm sure you would prefer another day for your Faika's wedding,' she said precariously.

He blinked confusedly.

It was an expression that encapsulated the extent of his need of her. She turned to hold him once more. She would wait a few moments before preparing breakfast and rushing off to the widower's.

'How tender you are!' Chaudry whispered, as he had last night.

Chapter Thirty

Momin found her at the foot of the staircase. Loose bandages, streaked with blood, entangled her chapped fingers. It was the first time he saw her without the bandages around her face. Her bare cheeks were matted in blood. Stunned, he shook her shoulders and in a quiet voice pleaded, 'Mrs Crow!' When she did not reply he folded his legs and sat beside the still body, listening to his heartbeat in contrast to her silence.

His mother was in the kitchen. From there the stairs could not be seen. For the first time in his life he longed to run to her, to ask openly for protection like the slobbering, bottle-drinking, peach-cheeked Faisal, who was upstairs being dressed for school by Saima. But he could not. A voice whispered that this was a test. He must think carefully.

Perhaps she had left a message?

He ran upstairs and entered the door he had left unlocked for her freedom. On the bedroll lay his drawings, arranged in a peculiar design that almost resembled a staircase. He could not restrain a smile. Did she like them?

Next to the pillow was what he looked for: 'No obstacles tonight, thank heaven.' He must ask Saima what obstacles meant. But he understood 'thank heaven' was her way of saying goodbye. She had gone to heaven.

Yet, when he returned to her, he grew queasy again, and had to struggle once more not to run for Malika. The house had never before seemed so large. There were, he counted, five people, excluding Mrs Saeed, the doorman, driver and his numerous garden friends, around him. Still he was alone. He held, then dropped, the Crow's icy claws. He deciphered a scrawl on one of the bloody bandage strips between them. Tugging it loose, he first noticed how bad it smelled. Then he read: '"The thin moonlit air echoes with jaws."'

The Crow was becoming as incomprehensible to him as his mother. Frowning, he tucked the tattered cloth into his shirt pocket, for Saima to explain later. From the pocket he removed a bit of paper doubled over several times into a tiny square and opened it. There was the Crow's eyelash. He recalled how it had fallen on him yesterday while she slept. He placed a finger to her eyelid. It did not quiver as it had then.

If the woman upstairs was the dead Mrs Saeed, how could she die again? What was death? Did ghosts die? Where was heaven?

His discomfort grew when no eyelash fell onto his crooked, henna-smeared, patiently extended finger. If only her skin weren't so blue.

Malika was making the Crow's breakfast. Soon he would not have to sit here alone trembling. She would come to him. Till then, he squatted with soldierly resolve, fighting back his tears, shooing away with his flaming orange hands the voice that kept repeating: this is not right.

He thought of his beloved Saima, and of the many brave boys whose stories she had brought into his world. At a moment like this what would she read him? He decided it would be the one about the feisty smidgen of a fellow, smaller than a dragonfly, who had accidentally fallen into a house of cold, blue-skinned giants. They used him as bait for mice and other squirmy creatures. He liked the picture of the fish that rescued him.

Momin turned his head in the direction of the windows, to the rose bed outside, barely visible from his position at the bottom of the stairs. If he leaned a bit, he could glimpse the top loop of the pond, where the minnows were. In the spring, according to the man who had helped him with the pond, the fish would multiply. The water lilies and roses would bloom. He would plant other flowers in the rockery for the moles to scamper through.

There was a lot to look forward to. Saima was happy. She was going to be a writer! He would go to school and make her proud.

He tried to think of other things to distract him, like his mother. He was glad she had returned to this house. She was all right, if only she did not keep hugging him. And his father. He was not exactly all right. Thinking of him made him fearful again.

He thought of the story of the little fellow. Ultimately, he was returned to the witch who had created him. Saima had explained how this cycle was like a birth. She had said birth was the opposite of death, and something had registered then. It meant because the boy was brave it ended well for him. This felt right.

Behind him sounded a loud crash. He turned abruptly. Malika's face was distended in a scream, a scream that at first he could not hear, so overcome was he by the terror in her eyes. It confirmed his fear: the Crow should not be here, lying with a still heart at the foot of the stairs without her mask. She should be flying in the square of glass above her room. What would happen now?

The Crow's Cerelac breakfast lay splattered at his mother's twitching feet in blobs. But this did not seem to be why she screamed. He could hear the shrill sound now. It said, 'Get up! Get up! You can't die!' It said to him, almost accusingly (but what had *he* done?): 'Your father! Oh, your dear father!'

Later, when Saima explained the word 'echo' from the Crow's last note, he would think of this moment, when everything ceased existing outside of the anguished cry.

READ MORE IN PENGUIN

In every corner of the world, on every subject under the sun, Penguin represents quality and variety—the very best in publishing today.

For complete information about books available from Penguin—including Puffins, Penguin Classics and Arkana—and how to order them, write to us at the appropriate address below. Please note that for copyright reasons the selection of books varies from country to country.

In India: Please write to *Penguin Books India Pvt. Ltd. 11 Community Centre, Panchsheel Park, New Delhi 110017*

In the United Kingdom: Please write to *Dept JC, Penguin Books Ltd. Bath Road, Harmondsworth, West Drayton, Middlesex, UB7 ODA. UK*

In the United States: Please write to *Penguin Putnam Inc., 375 Hudson Street, New York, NY 10014*

In Canada: Please write to *Penguin Books Canada Ltd. 10 Alcorn Avenue, Suite 300, Toronto, Ontario M4V 3B2*

In Australia: Please write to *Penguin Books Australia Ltd. 487, Maroondah Highway, Ring Wood, Victoria 3134*

In New Zealand: Please write to *Penguin Books (NZ) Ltd. Private Bag, Takapuna, Auckland 9*

In the Netherlands: Please write to *Penguin Books Netherlands B.V., Keizersgracht 231 NL-1016 DV Amsterdom*

In Germany : Please write to *Penguin Books Deutschland GmbH, Metzlerstrasse 26, 60595 Frankfurt am Main, Germany*

In Spain: Please write to *Penguin Books S.A., Bravo Murillo, 19-1'B, E-28015 Madrid, Spain*

In Italy: Please write to *Penguin Italia s.r.l., Via Felice Casati 20, 1-20104 Milano*

In France: Please write to *Penguin France S.A., 17 rue Lejeune, F-31000 Toulouse*

In Japan: Please write to *Penguin Books Japan. Ishikiribashi Building, 2-5-4, Suido, Tokyo 112*

In Greece: Please write to *Penguin Hellas Ltd, dimocritou 3, GR-106 71 Athens*

In South Africa: Please write to *Longman Penguin Books Southern Africa (Pty) Ltd, Private Bag X08, Bertsham 2013*

Moth Smoke
Mohsin Hamid

'An irresistibly engaging adventure and a searching portrait of contemporary young people in Pakistan … Confiding, witty, self-lacerating, arrogant and humble, and unfailingly convincing.'

—Joyce Carol Oates

The year is 1998, the summer of Pakistan's nuclear tests, and Darashikoh Shezad has just managed to lose his job in Lahore. As the economy crumbles around him, his electricity is cut off, and the jet set parties behind high walls, Daru takes the bright steps of falling for his best friend's wife and giving heroin a try. This is the story of his decline.

'"People don't believe in consequences anymore," says one of Mohsin Hamid's extraordinary characters. Not often does one find a first novel that has the power of imagination and skill to orchestrate personal and public themes of these consequences and achieve a chord that reverberates in one's mind. This novel does … This writer uncovers what people want to ignore about themselves.'

—Nadine Godimer

Ice-Candy-Man
(Now filmed as *1947*)
Bapsi Sidhwa

Few novels have caught the turmoil of the Indian subcontinent during Partition with such immediacy, such wit and tragic power.

Bapsi Sidhwa's *Ice-Candy-Man* is an intimate glimpse into events as they tear apart the world of Lenny, a young Parsee girl growing up in the pungent, busybodying city of Lahore.

'*Ice-Candy-Man* deserves to be ranked amongst the most authentic and best [books] on the partition of India.'
—Khushwant Singh

'Bapsi Sidhwa's capacity for bringing an assortment of characters vividly to life is enviable. She has given us in *Ice-Candy-Man* a memorable book, one that confirms her reputation as Pakistan's finest English language novelist.'
—*The New York Times Book Review*

'[Sidhwa] has told a sweet and amusing tale filled with the worst atrocities imaginable; she has concocted a girlishly romantic love story which is driven by the most militant feminism; above all, she has turned her gaze upon the domestic comedy of a Pakistani family in the 1940s and somehow managed to evoke the great political upheavals of the age.'
—*The Washingtom Post*

The Pakistani Bride
Bapsi Sidhwa

Zaitoon, a new bride, is desperately unhappy in her marriage and is contemplating the ultimate escape—the one from which there is no return.

Zaitoon, an orphan, is adopted by Qasim, who has left the isolated hill town where he was born and made a home for the two of them in the glittering, decadent city of Lahore. As the years pass Qasim makes a fortune but grows increasingly nostalgic about his life in the mountains. Impulsively, he promises Zaitoon in marriage to a man of his tribe. But for Zaitoon, giving up the civilized city life she remembers to become the bride of this hard, inscrutable husband proves traumatic to the point where she decided to run away, though she knows that by the tribal code the punishment for such an act is death.

'Sidhwa shows a marvellous feel for imagery—at a breathless pace she weaves her exotic cliffhanger from passion, power, lust, sensuality, cruelty and murder.'

—*Financial Times*

Blasphemy
Tehmina Durrani

'To me, my husband was my son's murderer. He was also my daughter's molester. A parasite nibbling on the Holy Book...'

Tehmina Durrani made her sensational literary debut in 1991 with her controversial autobiography, *My Feudal Lord.*

Blasphemy, her next major work, promises to generate the same degree of excitement. Set in South Pakistan, the novel inspired by a true story, is a searing study of evil; an uncompromising look at the distortion of Islam by predatory religious leaders. In prose of great power and intensity, the author tells the tragic story of the beautiful Heer, brutalized and corrupted by Pir Sain, the man of God, whom she is married to when barely fifteen. But the nightmare she is locked into is not hers alone; it affects the entire clan that owes allegiance to the pir. In the pir's haveli, unspeakable horrors are perpetrated every day and every night, all in the name of Allah. Sucked into the fetid hell of her lord's making, Heer loses her dignity, her freedom, even her humanity, till a terrible resolution gives her back to herself.

'The enduring impression of this book is it sustained capacity to shock the reader ... You turn the pages, compelled to read on.'

—*Biblio*